THE
POWER
STORE

THE MANAGER

VALERIE ERICKSON

ISBN: 978-1-7168-9271-4 (sc)
ISBN: 978-1-7168-9269-1 (e)

Library of Congress Control Number: 2020910023

Lulu Publishing Services rev. date: 06/02/2020

This book is dedicated to God,
who gave me the idea for this story.

CHARACTER SHEET

K eep track of the characters you meet by writing their names and adding a description!

_____

_____

_____

_____

_____

_____

_____

_____

_____

_____

_____

_____

_____

_____

PROLOGUE

"Have you ever wished you had super powers? Have you ever wanted to be able to do things that others couldn't do? To feel special and set apart? To be, a hero?

"I'm the Manager. I want to welcome you to my store, where we have more powers than you have ever dreamed. Get your power today!"

That's what the advertisement said. It was so far from the truth.

CHAPTER 1

THE ADVERTISEMENT

I was getting off the bus with my two best friends, Nick and Cody. We were heading home from West End High School. That was when we first saw the advertisement. It definitely caught our attention. Who *wouldn't* want powers? After gazing at it for a few minutes, we started to discuss which powers we would want.

"I would want to be superstrong, like the Hulk!" Nick shouted excitedly. He had always been picked on by his older brothers. He was short for his age, although his parents said he hadn't had his growth spurt yet. He wore hand-me-downs from all five of his older brothers and walked slouched over. He was a good friend but easily lost his temper when anyone messed with him or his friends.

"I'd want super-good looks!" answered Cody. He was the stereotypical nerd, with big thick glasses and a calculator and pens in his iron-pressed, collared shirt. And he was always carrying a book around that was way too big for his size.

I thought for a moment. I was the most average of the group. I received good grades without trying much. I wasn't particularly athletic, but I could keep up. I never wanted to attract attention to myself and didn't mind being in the background.

"Jay, what about you?" Nick asked.

"I wouldn't mind being invisible."

Nick and Cody snickered.

"You already are invisible," Nick retorted, laughing.

We continued walking down the street, discussing other powers we'd want and what it would be like. We arrived at our cul-de-sac less than a mile from our school. We usually hang out after school, until our parents called us home. But our end-of-the-year English papers were due Friday. We all knew it would be a good idea to start writing.

Nick and Cody waved goodbye to me and headed into their houses. As I walked home, my thoughts focused on the advertisement for powers. *How did that even work? Was there a magician? Did it require surgery? Was it a hoax? Nothing like that could actually be real, could it?*

Slam went the door.

"Jay? Is that you, honey?" shouted someone from down the hall.

"Hi, Mom. It's me." I dropped my backpack behind the front door, slowly ambled into the living room, kicked off my shoes, and dropped onto the couch.

"Jay, what's the matter? Are you all right?" I heard a soft, comforting voice behind me. I slowly turned my head and saw my mother's face peering at me. I gave her a thumbs-up, and she nodded as if understanding that I just needed some space.

I heard the squeak of her wheelchair maneuver out of the room. My mother, Georgia, was a loving and understanding mother. She had been a high school teacher at the school I attended. She taught until the car accident five years ago, which left her paralyzed from the waist down. Anyone could have gotten depressed, but my mom was just happy to be alive. During her time in the hospital, my father and I made some modifications to the house to make it more wheelchair friendly.

After a few minutes, I got up from the couch and headed to her sewing room, where she took the term "hobby" to a whole new level. I gazed at my mom, amazed she was working away as happy as could be. It almost seemed as if she didn't realize she was in a wheelchair. She looked up and saw my pondering look.

"How was school today, honey?" she asked as she continued to hand stitch beads on a dress.

"Okay," I replied without enthusiasm.

"What did you learn today?" she continued as if she didn't notice.

"Nothing much. I got an A on my math quiz."

"That's wonderful! You definitely have a good brain." She smiled proudly. "What else did you learn?"

"I have an English paper due. I should probably start working on it," I mumbled sheepishly.

"Sweetheart, do you mean the paper that was assigned over a month ago?" She turned to me with a sincere smile.

As a teacher, my mom had created the assignment of the reflective paper that came at the end of the school year. She wanted her students to have established some sort of goal for their lives by the time they finished their junior year of high school. Unfortunately for me, that was this current year.

We both knew she had warned me to work on the paper, but I kept procrastinating. I half-smiled back, picked up my backpack, and walked to my room. I found the paper detailing the assignment and read it as I sat at my desk.

"Who do you want to be? What are your goals or aspirations?

When you see yourself five years in the future, whom do you hope to see? Write a three- to five-page descriptive essay on your goals for the future. Explain three goals or characteristics you hope to develop and how you plan to achieve them."

I turned on my computer and opened up a Word document.

Who do I want to be? I wondered.

My thoughts wandered to the events of the day, Cody getting teased, Nick losing his temper and ending up in the principal's office, and then the walk home. I started thinking about the advertisement we saw. An idea slowly entered my head, and I started to type.

I continued typing through the creaking of the garage door announcing the arrival of my dad. I kept typing, even through Mom calling me to dinner.

Knock, knock. "Jay, did you hear your mother call us to dinner?" My dad poked his head into my room.

I finally looked up from my computer screen and saw my dad. Graham was a tall man who looked like an older version of myself. He ran his own business, selling games and educational toys. My friends and I loved it when he came home with new items to check out.

"Jay, it's time for dinner. Would you come to the table, please?" my dad asked.

I looked up at the Darth Vader clock on my shelf. I was surprised when I saw how late it was. I quickly turned back to my computer. *I typed four pages?*

"Sure, Dad. I'll be right there."

I saved my file and walked to the kitchen. It was Wednesday, which meant it would be my favorite meal of the week, lasagna!

Mom was an excellent cook, and the accident did not deter her from making the best homemade lasagna.

"So Jay, how's your paper going?" my mom asked.

"It's going really well," I replied. "I was inspired today when I was walking home with Nick and Cody."

"What inspired you?" Mom continued her investigation.

"We saw this advertisement at the bus stop. It talked about having powers. We thought about the different powers we wanted, and I thought of some that would be cool to have."

"I'm not sure that the assignment is about powers," Mom said.

"I know, but it just asks, 'Who do you want to be?' What if I want to be a superhero when I grow up?"

My parents exchanged glances. Dad asked, "What power would you want?"

I hesitated and then replied, "I would want the power to heal people. Wouldn't it be great if I could heal you, Mom?"

My parents smiled.

"That's very kind, son. I think that sounds like a great paper. Don't you, dear?" Dad asked Mom.

"I think that would be a great power to have," Mom responded.

I was confused. My parents didn't tell me how ridiculous it would be or how it could never happen. They just accepted what I said.

After dinner, I went back to my room and closed the door. I sat back at my computer and continued to work. I finished the paper, printed it, and then lay down on my bed. I wondered what it would be like if the Power Store were real. I closed my eyes and instantly started to dream of powers.

CHAPTER 2

DREAM JOBS

A t 7:29 a.m., I met up with my friends, and we started walking to school.

After a few blocks, Cody asked, "What did you write for your paper?"

"I wrote out a few jobs I wanted," Nick replied. "Professional boxer, MMA fighter, heavyweight champion ..."

Cody and I chuckled. Of course Nick would want to be known as a fighter. Having as many older brothers as he did, you don't survive unless you learn a few fighting and dodging techniques. Whenever Cody was bullied, Nick would always be there to pound them. He would even go up against guys twice his size.

They stared at me and waited for my answer. "I finished mine," I replied. "I want to be a doctor, so I can help heal people."

Nick and Cody stopped abruptly. I turned, wondering what was the matter.

Cody replied, "You do know that means you'll be in school for the next, uh, twenty years?"

I nodded. "I like school. I want to help people, like my mom. Wouldn't that be awesome if she could walk again?"

Nick and Cody sighed. They remembered how difficult it was for my dad and me after my mom's car accident.

Just then we heard the bus brakes squeal behind us and saw Kelly hop off. She was the only girl who could tolerate us. She was short, slightly awkward, and a bit clumsy. But she had so much confidence that it was as if she didn't notice.

"Hey, guys!" Kelly called happily.

"Hey, Kelly," we replied.

"Let's get to class. We don't want to be late." Kelly scampered off as if she were on her way to Disneyland.

The day passed uneventfully. The bell rang, signaling the end of school. We walked home. When we reached our corner, Nick went home to work on his paper, while Cody and I proceeded to Cody's house.

In his room, Cody had one wall papered with brochures to Ivy League schools. On the other side of his room hung the periodic table of elements. On the back was his famous tribute to *Star Wars*. It began as a few LEGO sets and a poster here and there but slowly evolved into an epic retelling of the story.

We played Pokémon until I needed to get home. When I arrived home, my dad was already at the dinner table. I sat down at my spot.

"So have you thought any more about the summer?" Dad asked.

"I guess I'll work at your store," I replied.

It was a pretty simple job: help customers, unpack shipments, and restock shelves. After dinner, I returned to my room and tried to work on my homework, but my mind kept wandering. I wasn't able to stay focused. Eventually, I gave up and went to bed.

The next day, as we walked home from school, we discussed

which video games we would play that night. We passed by that same advertisement for powers. It caused us to pause.

"I don't get it," Cody wondered out loud. "If there actually were a Power Store, wouldn't we see everyone flying around, using the Force, or reading people's minds?"

Nick and I chuckled at him.

"I'm not sure how it would work. There must be some sort of rule that prevents you from showing off your power. Think of the panic it would cause if people saw you flying," Nick responded thoughtfully.

How would that work? I wondered to myself.

CHAPTER 3

SUMMER!

"Yeah ha!" "Woohoo!" "Yay!" "All right!" "Freedom!" were a few of the celebratory yells heard throughout the whole school. Summer had arrived.

As we paraded through the halls for the last time that year, Ms. James, our English teacher, stopped me and asked to chat with me about my paper. Nick and Cody glanced at me, but I waved them on and said I'd meet up with them soon. I cautiously walked with her back to her classroom.

"I really enjoyed your paper, Jay. What made you think of that topic?" Ms. James asked innocently.

"Well, I wanted to do what I could to help people. I figured being a surgeon would be a good way," I answered honestly.

"That's a wonderful goal. But I was talking about the power. Where did you get an idea like that?"

Ms. James was asking me about powers? "Uh, we saw an advertisement for a store that sells powers. I thought it would be a funny thing to write about." I was very confused.

"What do you think it would be like to have the power to heal?" Ms. James asked, seeming anxious to hear my answer.

11

I was unsure how to respond. "I guess it would be cool. It would help me become a good doctor. I'd try to heal my mom and any of my friends who got hurt."

Ms. James was smiling. "Good for you. Have an amazing summer, Jay," Ms. James replied. She returned to her desk and started packing her things. I sort of stood there and slowly realized that I was allowed to leave. As I walked out of the classroom, I noticed Nick and Cody sitting on a bench.

"What happened, Jay?" Cody inquired.

"Did you get in trouble?" Nick asked.

"No, she just asked me about my paper."

"Man, I thought that having a teacher as a mom you'd never get in trouble. Shouldn't you be the perfect student?" Nick asked jokingly.

I smiled and led my two friends away from the school. All our fellow students had already left. Papers and notebooks were strewn about the campus. It was a great feeling to be done with another year of school.

We walked to purchase our weekly pizza and doughnuts. As we returned home with our bounty of junk food, Nick and Cody started talking about their summer plans. I got lost in thought about my conversation with Ms. James. *What did she mean by her questions? She didn't talk to anyone else about their papers.*

Nick and Cody stopped walking and looked at me. Apparently they had asked me a question that I hadn't heard.

"What's bothering you? Was it something Ms. James said?" Cody asked. He always knew when something was bothering me, and he was not likely to give up until he figured out what.

"Yeah, it was something she said about my paper."

"Wow, was it really that bad?" Nick laughed at his own joke.

"Ignore him," Cody said dismissively. "What did she say?"

"Well, you remember the first time we saw the power ad?" They nodded. "I wrote about a power in my paper, and Ms. James asked me why I would want that power."

"That's weird. Why would she care about that?" Cody asked. "I'm not sure."

Cody seemed to be considering this, and eventually Nick changed the subject.

I told my friends that I needed to go home quickly and that I would meet up with them later.

As I opened the door, I yelled, "Mom?"

"In here, honey," I heard my mother respond from the next room.

I also heard another woman's voice, but I couldn't tell who it was. I poked my head around the corner. I saw my mom sitting with a cup of tea, speaking with—Ms. James? That was unexpected. Then I remembered that she and my mom were old friends. Still, it was weird coming home to see your teacher there.

Ms. James turned around. "Hi, Jay. I was just catching up with your mom."

I nodded and Ms. James stood up. "I think this could be a great opportunity. I'm glad you've chosen to do this." Ms. James grabbed her purse from the back of her chair and walked out.

Mom looked up at me, and I gave her a questioning look. "Gina was just giving me some tips on healthy living," she explained.

It felt weird to hear my mom call my teacher by her first name.

"Jay, your father and I would like to take you somewhere tomorrow for your birthday," she said quickly.

Yes! I thought. That was one added benefit to the end of school. It always came right before my birthday.

"May I invite Nick and Cody?"

"Well, honey, we thought this time it would be just you, your dad, and I. You can see your friends after."

I thought about it and finally agreed. I dropped my backpack in my room and headed back out to Nick's house. That evening, we talked about summer, watched a movie, and pigged out on pizza and doughnuts.

Around 11 o'clock, I walked back to my house, slipped inside, and headed to bed.

CHAPTER 4

AN UNEXPECTED BIRTHDAY PRESENT

"Are you sure you can't tell me where we're going?" I asked for the fifth time.

"Absolutely not," replied my dad from the driver's seat. "This is a surprise for your birthday."

"You're going to love it, Jay," Mom responded as she looked back at me.

I was so confused. I woke up to my favorite breakfast: apple-cinnamon waffles with apple syrup. Then my parents asked me to get ready for the day. I had no idea what they meant by that, so I just did so without asking questions. My dad and I helped place my mom in the car, got in, and started driving. I knew we were somewhere north of town, but I had no idea where we were going.

What birthday present could they have for me? I hadn't been allowed to take my friends or ask any questions. I decided to stop worrying about it and tried to make some sense of where we were.

About fifteen minutes later, we exited the freeway. *Where are we?* I was really confused. After driving through a few streets, my parents finally parked in a huge parking lot.

Surrounding the lot was a SaveMart, a Chinese restaurant, and a few small stores. At the end was a tiny store that looked no bigger than our kitchen. That was where my dad was wheeling my mother. I followed them.

When we approached the store, I read the store name. "Wait. How do you guys know about this place? It's real?" I asked incredulously.

They both smiled at me and gestured for me to go inside. When I opened the door, I was struck by how small it was. On the walls were racks of posters. There were five rows on the wall and thirty or more posters in each row. At the end of the rows was a small table with a cash register. Behind the cash register sat a short, unassuming man. He looked up at me as if he expected our arrival.

"Welcome to the Power Store! Please come in. I'm the Manager. Who might you be?"

I froze, unsure of what to do. "I'm Jay."

"Pleased to meet you, Jay. These must be your parents. It's a pleasure. So I assume that you called for your son."

My mom nodded. "Yes. It's his seventeenth birthday, and we wanted to give him something very special."

Mom called the store?

"Well, you've certainly come to the right place. If you would, please step into my office. Jay, why don't you take a look around, and see what looks right for you?"

I was even more confused. Look around at what? See what looks right? My mom and dad passed by me and followed the Manager into his office. The door shut, and I was by myself.

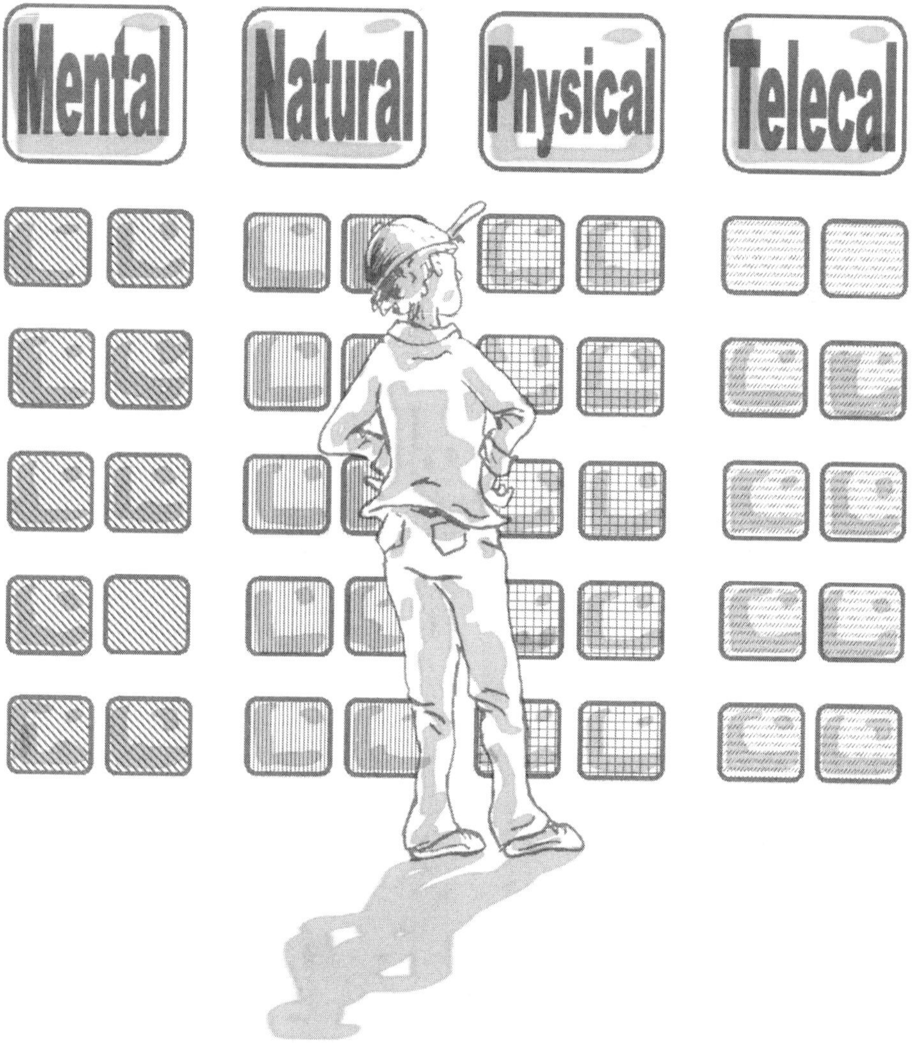
Mental
Natural
Physical
Telecal

I started to read the words on the walls: "Emotional," "Mental," "Natural," "Physical," "Telecal." I had no idea what Telecal meant, so I started looking through that row of posters: Telecommunication, Telekinesis, Teleport, Telepath. Each poster had a large word and some small writing below it. I read one of the posters.

"Telekinesis: Ability to move things without touching them." *I guess that's like the Force.*

I kept looking through the other rows and saw other random powers listed: Animal, Breathe, Care, Calm, Control, Detox, Disappear, Dormeatas. *Dormeatas? What does that mean?* I read the description on the side. "Dormeatas: ability Ability to eat while you sleep."

Eating in your sleep? Who would want that *power?*

I kept reading the other powers: Earth, Flight, Ghost, Grow, Halt, Heal, Hear, Influence, Interesting.

I paused briefly and returned to Heal. "Heal: Ability to heal the physical body. With one touch, you will be able to heal any injury." At the bottom, in very small writing, was, "Not all injuries can be healed."

The power to Heal? I wondered what that would be like. I could do anything I wanted and be able to heal myself. I could be dressed up as a doctor, visit patients, and heal them! Would I be able to heal my mom?

The door opened and out came my parents, followed by the Manager. They were all laughing as if they had known each other for years.

"Well, have you made a decision?" My parents looked at me expectantly. The Manager was looking at me intently as well.

"I'm not, um, I don't know what's going on," I admitted.

"Not to worry, Jay. You see, this is a very special store. We offer powers to our clients. All the powers listed here could be yours. Your parents have agreed to allow you to have a power, should you wish to take it."

I turned to my parents with a questioning look.

"This is this real? Am I being pranked?" I asked honestly.

Mom smiled. "Of course this is real, Jay. The Manager was explaining how a team of scientists has developed serums that give people powers. Happy birthday!"

It slowly sank in. My parents were giving me a power for my birthday.

"How long does it last?" I asked.

"Well, the trial period will give you a limited amount of the power, free of charge. Then if you would like, we can give you an unlimited supply." The Manager turned toward my parents and asked, "How about we start him off with a trial, and then he can make a more informed decision?"

My parents nodded at his suggestion.

"So how about it, Jay? Is there a power that looks appealing to you?" the Manager asked curiously.

I glanced back at all the posters. All of those powers were at my fingertips to do with and use as I wanted.

"Jay, you take your time. Your mom and I are going to stand outside, and you come out when you're all finished," Dad said as he started wheeling my mom toward the door.

The Manager nodded and opened the door for them. Then he turned toward me. "I know this may be difficult for you to understand, Jay. I had quite a difficult time believing it myself when I first heard about it. Here's how it works. Tell me which power you'd like. I'll give you a sample portion, which should last you about a month, if you choose to use it properly.

Then you can come back and try another or continue with that power." The Manager gestured to all of the posters. "Which shall it be, Jay?"

"Heal. I want Heal," I said suddenly.

"Excellent choice! I'll be right back with the sample." He hurried off to his office and came back with a test tube full of light-blue liquid. He held it out to me.

What do I have to lose? I took the tube and drank it all in one gulp. It didn't taste like anything, and I didn't feel any different. I looked up at the Manager.

"Jay, you have selected an excellent power. I'll expect to hear from you soon. Go change the world!" The Manager held out his hand to me and gestured toward the door.

I walked out and heard the door close behind me.

That was it?

I didn't see my parents at first. They were probably laughing at me for believing it was real. I walked toward the car and saw my parents waiting inside.

"So what's it like, Jay?" Dad inquired as I approached.

"Ha, ha, very funny," I grumbled as I got into the car.

Mom and Dad gave me confused looks. "It didn't work?" Mom asked me.

I abruptly took my mom's hand. "Can you feel your toes, Mom?" I demanded.

She looked a little surprised. "No, Jay. Why? Which power did you choose?"

"Heal," I answered with a sigh.

"Oh, sweetheart, that's a great idea. Unfortunately, that power wouldn't be able to heal me," she responded, patting my hand.

"Maybe we'll have to test it out another way," Dad piped in.

Test it out? What was going on with my parents? They seriously believed that something like this could actually exist?

I was in a bad mood during the car ride home. I thought that this would be something wonderful. I could heal my mom and then start healing those who were terminally ill.

When we arrived home, I walked over to Cody's house. Cody's mom answered the door and said, "Good morning, Jay! Come on in. Happy birthday! I hope you're having a good day so far. Cody isn't feeling too well, but I'm sure he'd like the company." She returned to the kitchen, leaving me in the doorway.

Cody isn't feeling well? Hmm. I walked to Cody's room and found him in his bed, watching the Discovery Channel.

"Hey, man, happy birthday." *Cough, cough.* "Sorry. Great way to start summer vacation, isn't it?" Cody spoke through his coughs.

I cautiously approached my friend and took his hand.

"What are you doing?" Cody demanded.

"Hold still," I responded quietly. Cody, looking very perplexed, sat still while I gripped his hand. "How do you feel?"

Cody sat up. "I feel, fine. My cough is all gone! Wait, what did you do?"

I got a huge smile on my face. It really *worked*! "Dude, let's go get Nick!" I ran out of the room.

"Wait, I'm still in my pajamas!" Cody yelled.

Less than a minute later, we left.

"Cody, where are you going?" his mom called after him.

"I feel fine, Mom. I'll see you later!" Cody shouted back.

We got to Nick's house and dragged him out of bed.

"Whoa, what's going on? Hey, it's my first chance to sleep in," Nick complained.

"Come on, man. We're going to the tree!" I said to my friend who was still half asleep.

"All right, I'm coming. Sheesh, some friends you are."

Soon, all of us were running frantically to the park. There was a certain tree at there that served as our meeting place. Anytime there was something serious that we needed to talk about, we met at the tree. This slowly evolved into code for, "Something major happened!"

We all arrived at the tree and collapsed on the ground. "All right, geniuses. What's so important that you had to wake me up?" Nick yelled angrily.

I put my hand on Nick's shoulder. "How do you feel, Nick?" I asked.

"That's weird. I'm not tired anymore. What did you do?"

"You had better start at the beginning, Jay," Cody said, sitting down next to Nick.

I started by reminding them about the advertisement. I told them about Ms. James, what my mother said, my parents' birthday gift for me, and the strange store they took to.

Cody had an inquisitive look on his face. "Did you use your power on me this morning?" I nodded.

"What was the matter with you?" Nick asked Cody.

"I woke up with a 102 degree temperature and have been coughing up gunk all morning while you were sleeping in. Thank you for your concern. Now I feel totally fine," Cody responded triumphantly.

"So you have the power to Heal?" Nick's eyes were wide open in shock.

"Yeah, that's the one I chose." My friends were a mix of stunned and impressed.

"How long do you have it for?" Nick asked.

"The guy—or the Manager—gave me the sample and said that it was based on how I used it."

"I wonder what else you can heal. Let's test it!" Nick stood up suddenly and started climbing the tree next to us. He kept climbing until he got all the way to the top, about twenty feet up.

"What are you doing, Nick?" I asked worriedly. Nick was not a fan of heights.

"I'm going to jump, and you're going to heal me!"

"Nick, that's insane. You're going to break both of your legs!" I yelled.

"Seriously, let's start off with small stuff, like a cut or a bruise," Cody suggested.

"Three, two, one!" Nick let go of the tree, and Cody and I looked away. A few seconds later, we heard a sickening thud followed by a blood-curdling scream from Nick. His shins looked like they had been snapped in half.

"Come on, Jay. You gotta heal him," Cody begged.

"What? Are you crazy? I haven't done that before!" I yelled in protest.

"Jay, he's crying and screaming. He's in a lot of pain. You have to try!" Cody was trying to hold Nick down. He was writhing in pain and wailing. I grabbed his hand and concentrated.

Soon, Nick stopped screaming. We looked at his legs. They were slowly straightening out.

After about ten seconds of silence, Nick sat up and looked at us. "Did it work?" he asked.

I punched him in the nose. "Don't you *ever* do *anything* like that again! Do you hear me?" I never yelled or punched anyone. Nick knew I was angry.

"Ow, my nose," Nick complained.

"Good! I'm not going to heal it," I retorted.

Cody, who was a bit more calm, asked Nick, "How are your legs?"

Nick stood up and walked around. "They're fine. This is awesome! Although my nose really does hurt."

I sighed. Nick could be such an idiot sometimes. I placed my hand on his nose, and soon the blood stopped. Nick wiggled his nose a bit and smiled.

"I'm sorry for jumping out of a tree, dude. I was just so anxious to see what you could do."

"Well next time you have any bright ideas about mangling yourself, I will not be there to save you!"

Nick smiled. Cody was thoughtful.

"So what should we test next?" Nick asked with a devious grin. We started laughing and decided to keep testing my new power.

CHAPTER 5

TESTING JAY'S POWER

"So the sample will last a month?" Nick asked as he was enjoying an ice cream. The first day of summer must be accompanied with ice cream.

"Yup," I replied through mouthfuls of strawberry cheesecake ice cream, "if I choose to use it properly."

"I wonder what *that* means," said Cody.

"Who cares? One month of healing power. That sounds like the best birthday present ever! Your parents are so cool," Nick exclaimed.

My parents? "Oh, shoot, I never thanked them." I quickly wolfed down the rest of my cake cone and ran back to my house.

"I wonder how his parents found that store," Cody wondered aloud.

"I wonder what other powers exist," Nick replied.

I ran as fast as I could toward my house. However, I quickly got a stomachache from all the ice cream I had just eaten. I paused briefly and put my hand on my stomach. Almost instantly, I felt 100 percent and continued running.

About five minutes later, I reached my house, opened the door, and called for my parents. Both of them were in the kitchen and looked up, wondering what was wrong.

I gave them both a huge hug. "What's the matter, Jay?" my mom asked.

"Nothing. I just never said thank you for my wonderful birthday present."

My dad chuckled. "You're welcome, son. We know that you'll choose to use it properly."

I looked at them and asked, "How did you know about that store?"

"Oh, honey, just because we're old doesn't mean we don't see advertisements, especially when they're for something amazing."

"But you called the store, and the Manager was expecting us."

"That's how the store works, Jay," Dad explained. "You call the number to make an appointment, and the Manager works with his clients one-on-one."

"May I have the number?"

"Are you thinking of getting the full-time power?" Mom questioned.

"Well, yeah. I mean, this is seriously the greatest present I have ever gotten. I want it to last."

"That's fine, Jay. But remember, there is a cost to the powers," Dad cautioned.

"But the Manager said it was free."

"Yes, the sample comes free. But there is a heavy price if you choose to use the power improperly. How about this? Come back to us in one month. If you still want the number, we'll give it to you. Does that sound like a deal?" Dad asked.

I wondered what the heavy price would be. "Deal. Thanks, Dad. Thanks, Mom!" I ran back to my friends. I only had to stop once to heal myself as I ran back to meet my friends. They had already finished their ice cream and were waiting for me.

"Dude, did you run home and back in that short of time?" Nick asked with a questioning look.

"How long was I gone?"

"About fifteen minutes," Cody responded. "Did you use your power on yourself?"

"Only two times. I got a stomachache from running so fast."

Cody was taking notes. He was one of the few people who carried around a notebook.

"Mr. Smarty is writing all the facts on who and what you have healed," Nick explained.

That made sense. Out of the three of us, Cody was definitely the most meticulous at gathering and recording facts.

"So what's next? Should we advertise you? Oh, think of all the money we could make!" Nick leaned back in his chair, picturing all the things he would buy.

"I don't think that would fall under the category of using it properly. It shouldn't be used to make money. Let's go home. Maybe on the way we'll see if anyone's hurt."

As we walked home, we saw one of our neighbors on his bike, facing a bike ramp. "Hey, Ray," I called out. "Didn't your mom ground you from using your bike ramp?"

"Quiet!" Ray responded in a loud whisper. "My mom's not here, and she'll never know."

"You know she's just worried that you're going to break something," Cody stated responsibly.

"Aw, come on, guys. I saw this really awesome bike trick, and I know I can land it," Ray pleaded.

"Just try it quickly, and get the ramp in before your mom sees you," Nick urged him on. He winked at me, knowing that if anything did go wrong, I could fix it.

Ray sat on his bike and started pedaling. Soon, he flew up the ramp and started to do a backflip with his bike. He yelled out an enthusiastic holler. We wondered if he would make it. Unfortunately, he didn't.

Splat! He fell directly on his back, and his bike landed on top of him. Cody, Nick, and I ran over to him. He was coughing up blood and panicking.

"Is he dead?" Nick asked cautiously.

"No, he's breathing," Cody responded. "Jay, hurry up!"

I slowly squatted and picked up Ray's hand. A few seconds later, Ray quickly sat up.

"What did you do?" Ray demanded.

"Well," Cody struggled to find an explanation.

"You got knocked out. You almost made it but you landed on your back tire and fell backwards. How are you feeling?" I asked.

"I didn't get knocked out. I saw you. Why were you holding my hand?" Ray looked at me with a suspicious look.

Cody and I helped him up and he brushed himself off.

"You just had a really hard fall. You must have been seeing things," Nick said threateningly.

"No. I remember everything. I didn't flip right, and I fell hard on my back. You grabbed my hand, Jay, and I felt better instantly." Ray was convinced that he was telling the truth.

I abruptly grabbed Ray by the shirt. "Listen, Ray, if you *ever* tell anyone what happened, we'll tell your mom that you've been using your bike ramp."

"Chill, man. I'm not going to say anything. Just tell me, what happened?" Ray asked desperately.

I glanced over at Nick and Cody. Nick kind of shrugged, but Cody looked worried.

"Come on. Let's go inside. My mom got fudge bars yesterday." Ray ran into the garage to put away his bike. Cody, Nick, and I helped with the bike ramp. We followed Ray into his house.

"So what did you do?" Ray asked after handing everyone a fudge bar.

"You wouldn't believe me if I told you," I responded.

"Try me," Ray said confidently, taking a bite.

I sighed. "You have to promise not to tell *anyone*. Got it?" Ray nodded for me to continue. "My parents took me to this store that sells powers."

"The Power Store? Like the advertisement?" Ray could barely believe it.

"Yeah, that store. I got a power for my birthday. I chose Heal."

"Wow. So you can heal, like anything?" Ray's excitement grew.

"We've tested out a few things. I guess we'll have to add you to the log." I looked over at Cody, who was already carefully documenting.

"That's incredible. I didn't realize that was real."

"Neither did I. But seriously, Ray, you can't tell anyone," I reminded him.

"All right, all right. Wow, thanks for healing me. I would've gotten in so much trouble with my mom if we had to call an ambulance," Ray responded guiltily.

I noticed the time. "Oh, shoot! I gotta get home for dinner." Nick, Cody, and I walked out and waved goodbye to Ray.

A few minutes later, we arrived home. Inside were a few balloons and streamers hanging on the walls. My parents were in the kitchen, fixing dinner. They looked up and yelled, "Happy birthday!"

I had almost forgotten that it was still my birthday.

My parents had been making my favorite meal: steak, mashed potatoes, corn, green beans, and garlic bread. We all sat down together. Nick and Cody told them about the wonderful day we had with my power. They listened and asked questions about it. Everyone seemed to agree I chose a power that fit well.

After dinner, my parents pulled out a chocolate cake that looked like the Death Star.

After eating my cake, my friends and I went into the living room to play video games for a few hours. After they left, I walked out to where my parents were sitting. "Thank you, Mom and Dad. I had a really awesome birthday." I smiled.

"We're so glad, Jay. You know, we debated whether or not to get you a car—"

"No," I interrupted my father. "This was perfect!" I gave my parents a big hug.

"We love you, Jay. We know you're going to use this well," my mom responded.

I went to my room and thought about how I could use my power to help everyone.

CHAPTER 6

UNLIMITED SUPPLY

Three weeks of summer passed. I had gotten into the routine of working for my dad during the day and hanging out with my friends in the evening. We continued to log whom I healed. I had to be careful when to use my power because I did not want to attract attention to myself. I helped a few young kids at the playground, experimented on Cody and Nick, and healed myself a few times.

I came to depend on my power. A few times while working, I accidentally dropped a heavy box on my foot or got a paper cut. I healed myself before anyone noticed. Once or twice a customer came in feeling sick. I quietly healed them with a comforting pat on the back. Cody's notebook was slowly getting filled.

"It's going to be weird when the power runs out," I confessed to my friends.

"What are you talking about? When that happens, we'll just go back to the store and get the unlimited supply," Nick responded as if it were obvious.

"I'm not sure. I don't have a lot of money. Who knows how much something like this would cost?" I replied.

"It wouldn't hurt to ask. Are you feeling like it's running out?" Cody inquired.

"I'm not sure. It does take longer to heal things," I confessed.

Suddenly, Nick smacked his head hard against the table, causing us to jump. "Owwwww," Nick yelled as blood poured down his face.

I sighed and put my hand on my friend's nose. At first nothing happened. Then the blood slowly stopped flowing.

"You are an idiot, Nick," Cody said, smacking his head with his notebook.

"My nose still feels a little weird. Does it look all right?" Nick asked.

"It does look a little crooked," I admitted. I put my hand on his nose. A few seconds later, it straightened out.

"Hmm, maybe we could try to find this store," Cody considered.

"I could ask my parents for the address," I responded. We agreed that this was a good plan.

When we arrived at my house, we found my mom at her sewing table. "Hey, Mom. Would you give us the address of the Power Store?"

She stopped and looked at the three of us. "Are you all thinking of getting a power?"

We nodded. She smiled and wrote down an address. "Have fun, but be careful," she warned.

Address in hand, we discussed the quickest way to get to the store. Collectively, we had enough money for the three of us to ride the bus there and back. We walked over to the bus stop, waited for the right one, and then got on.

About a dozen people were on the bus. One older woman,

sitting in the middle, was coughing. No one else seemed to notice. I carefully brushed my hand on her shoulder as I walked by. Nick, Cody, and I sat in the row behind her. A few seconds later, she had another coughing fit. I cautiously put my hand on her shoulder. Pretty soon, she was breathing normally. Cody got out his notebook and documented the incident.

A few stops and thirty minutes later, I noticed the same parking lot that my parents took me to. I saw the SaveMart and told my friends that this was the place. We got off, walked across the parking lot, and found the small store. Nick and Cody seemed really excited as they read the name of the store.

"You'd think that a store selling powers would be a lot bigger," Nick said, scoffing.

I quietly opened the door and went in, and my friends followed. It was exactly the same as before. I pointed the posters out to my friends, who started reading through the different powers. I tiptoed to the back of the store. The Manager's office was cracked open, and I could hear him talking.

"Yes, just disappeared! I'm staring at the map now. This is the fifth green dot this month. That makes thirty who have disappeared. No, I haven't received any complaints."

There was no response, so I knew the Manager was on the phone.

"Well, all right," the Manager said. "Thank you for your attention to this matter. Goodbye." I heard him put the phone down, and I pretended to look at the different powers.

The Manager came out of his office and saw me standing there. "Welcome back, Jay." He gave me a hearty handshake. "I hope you enjoyed your experience with your power."

"Very much so, Manager, sir."

"No, no, it's just Manager. I see you brought some friends with you."

"This is Nick and Cody." I gestured to my friends who walked over.

They all shook hands and then the Manager welcomed us into his office. "So Jay, did you come back to try something else? Or did you want the full supply?" the Manager asked.

"Well, I'm not sure how much it costs. I don't have much," I confessed.

"Oh, don't worry. We don't deal in money here," the Manager exclaimed proudly. "We are what you might call a nonprofit business."

"How does this work then?" Nick asked.

"Let me explain to you boys. All our clients have an unlimited source of power. And this watch." The Manager showed us the watch. "It looks like an ordinary watch to anyone who sees it. But for the wearer, it shows a power meter. As long as the power is used for good and not for personal gain, the power meter remains in the green. When someone decides to use his or her power for selfish reasons, one of the green bars turns red." He showed us what looked like a simple wristwatch. But instead of a clock face, three green marks glowed. It reminded me of a WiFi symbol.

"What happens if all three bars turn red?" I asked cautiously.

"Oh, I'm sure that's not going to happen to you. I don't know of anyone that it has happened to. However, if that were to happen, the customer would go into debt. He would have to work off his debt, and then he'd be able to reset his watch."

"So, let me get this straight. I ask for an unlimited amount of a certain power. You give me the power and a watch, and I don't have to pay anything?" Nick asked skeptically.

"That is correct," the Manager replied. "You see, gentlemen, my boss is an extraordinary man. He and his team of scientists want to change the world. By giving out these powers, they hope to make the world a better place for everyone." The Manager looked very proud to work here.

"What are the rules?" Nick continued.

"There are a few basic rules, Nick. You can't use your power for selfish reasons or personal gain. That means no public displays of your power. We don't want to cause panic or mass hysteria among the people."

Nick nodded.

"Next, we caution against telling too many people. The reason that our store has been so successful is that not many people know we exist. We advertise in a few select locations and only have a handful of stores across the country. We like to expand slowly so we can monitor those who have powers. Finally, no one under seventeen may have a power." The Manager looked pointedly at me.

That was why it was such a big deal for my parents.

"So boys, which powers would you like to have?" The Manager stood up and gestured toward the store. Nick and Cody stood and left the office to view their options.

"How about you, Jay? Would you like to try a different power?"

"No, thank you. I really enjoyed healing."

"Excellent. I'll get everything ready as soon as your friends have made their choices." The Manager and I walked out to see what my friends were up to.

Cody spent the next hour methodically reading through every single power. He had to find the perfect one. Nick knew almost instantly as soon as he found the physical power, Strength.

Finally, Cody settled on the power called Memory, which would allow the user to remember everything that he or she had ever heard or read. I didn't think Cody needed this power because he already had an almost photographic memory.

The Manager got three watches and gave them to the Nicky, Cody, and I. He also held three syringes. One was labeled "Heal," another "Strength," and the last one "Memory."

"Whoa, whoa, whoa! You didn't say anything about a shot!" Nick backed away from the Manager. Nick did not like shots.

He smiled calmly. "I understand your hesitation, Nick. This is a small implant that holds the power."

"How big is the implant? Will you be able to see it?" Cody inquired.

"Not at all. It's as thin as a toothpick, and you won't notice it. I place it in your wrist, right below your hand." The Manager showed us his arm.

Nick was a little wary, so I offered to go first. I sat on the chair the Manager offered to me.

"Now relax. Just think of how you will use your power to help. There! All finished."

That's it?

The Manager handed me my watch. My wrist was a bit sore. I touched it with my other hand, and it instantly felt better. I put my watch on and saw that my power meter was completely green.

Cody went next and had no trouble either. I touched his wrist because his was also a bit uncomfortable.

Nick was still a bit apprehensive. Cody and I grabbed him and forced him to sit in the chair. "Come on, man, unlimited power! You'll never have to worry about how heavy your backpack is," I said, trying to convince Nick.

The Manager picked up the needle and put it in Nick's arm before he could struggle. I healed his wrist and let go of Nick's arm.

"Well, gentlemen, shall we try a test?" The Manager had an excited gleam in his eye. "Cody, let's start with you. I'm going to read a passage from Shakespeare. I'd like for you to repeat it back to me."

The Manager pulled a book from behind the cash register and read Hamlet's "To be or not to be" soliloquy. A minute later, he finished, and we looked expectantly at Cody.

"To be or not to be. That is the question: Whether 'tis nobler in the mind to suffer." He finished the entire speech without taking a breath. Nick and I dropped our jaws in awe. Cody looked at us smugly.

"Be careful what you say around me," he said proudly to Nick and me. "I won't forget it."

"Let's try your new power, Nick," the Manager suggested as he walked toward his office. We followed him, wondering what his test would look like. "I have this file cabinet I would love to move to the other side of my office." The Manager gestured toward it. It was as tall as Nick and wedged in the corner. Nick walked over to it, leaned it forward, and picked it up. It seemed like he was just picking up an empty cardboard box. He took the filing cabinet to the other side of the office and set it down with ease. We stared in disbelief.

"Pretty cool, huh?" Nick smiled proudly. He walked over to Cody and gave him a playful punch in the arm.

"Ow!" Cody yelled. "What was that for?"

"What? What did I do?" Nick asked anxiously.

"You broke my arm!" Cody howled in pain.

I stepped up and put my hand on Cody's arm. He stopped howling and punched Nick back.

"Is that normal?" I asked the Manager.

"Unfortunately, your powers may take some getting used to. The powers that you and Cody chose will be easier to hide. Nick will have to practice not using his power all the time. We wouldn't want him shattering someone's hand the next time he gives a handshake or accidentally breaking a door while opening it," the Manager warned.

"All right, I'll be careful. Sorry, Cody," Nick said sheepishly.

"Is there anything else we should know?" I asked.

"I think we're all set here. Feel free to visit whenever you have any questions or problems." He led us out of his office. "Now boys, go change the world!" The Manager waved at us as we left.

"I can't believe it. He just gives us powers, watches, and shows us the door?" Cody asked suspiciously.

"Who cares? I'm so strong! Just watch this." Nick ran over to a car and picked it up like it was a pillow.

"Nick, stop it," I yelled. "Put that down before someone sees you!"

"Sorry! I'm just excited. Nothing this cool has ever happened to me before." Nick set down the car gently. We heard a loud beep, and all of us checked our watches.

"Aw, man, already?" Nick's power meter had gone down one mark.

"At least you're still in the green," I commented.

"I guess so," Nick said disappointedly.

"It looks like you have two more strikes until you're in the red," I said.

"Yeah, you don't want to be in debt. Should we have asked exactly what that means?" Cody asked.

"Nah, we're not going to use our powers selfishly. Right, Nick?" I asked, glaring at Nick.

"I'll be good," Nick replied in surrender.

"Come on. We gotta catch the bus home," I said quickly.

Nick, Cody, and I jogged over to the bus stop. We got on the bus and headed home. On the trip, Cody started a new page for each of us so he could write all the times we used our powers. Beneath Nick's name, he wrote, "Selfishly used his strength to lift a car." At the end, he wrote, "Strike 1."

CHAPTER 7

TRAINING GROUNDS

"All right, lift slowly and hold as long as you can. Now!" Cody started his stopwatch as Nick held a car over his head. Cody, Nick, and I had been running extensive drills and tests to see the extent of our powers. We were sitting in the middle of a junkyard, with no one in sight. We thought this would be a good place for our tests.

"Anything?" I asked Nick.

"I'm good! I could do this all day," Nick yelled back, holding the car up with one hand.

"It seems that Nick has almost unlimited strength. He can pick up anything as if it were a piece of paper," Cody stated while writing more notes.

"I'm starting to get a little tired, though," Nick admitted.

"Describe it, please," Cody responded, still writing.

"My arms are a bit sore, and I feel like I've been awake for the past two days straight." He placed the car down in front of him and collapsed on the ground as Cody stopped his watch.

"No kidding. You held the car up for almost three minutes!" Cody exclaimed.

"Jay, could you give me a hand?" Nick asked weakly.

I walked over to my friend and helped him up. As Nick stood, he said, "All better! Now what?" he asked energetically.

Cody glared at me. "Jay, if you keep healing him, I won't ever be able to make accurate conclusions about his power."

"Sorry, man. He looked like he needed it," I admitted.

"Fine. Let's try another memory test." Cody handed me his notebook.

We were taking turns testing each other's abilities. Tests for Nick consisted of him holding heavy stuff over his head. I would heal him, and then Cody would memorize random bits of information. So far, he had learned the capitals of all the countries in the world and the names of their leaders. He memorized all the elements on the periodic table and all their scientific properties.

"Let's try pi," Cody said, standing in ready position.

"Sounds good. I'm in the mood for apple," Nick responded. Cody glared at him while Nick opened up his math book. Nick recited the first one hundred digits of pi.

Cody waited about ten seconds and then repeated, "3.14159265358979 ...," accurately saying each number in order.

"Oy, you're really gonna make me look stupid in school," Nick sighed dejectedly.

Cody, looking very smug, responded, "Let's try something harder."

"Want to memorize names of stars? The human DNA? Different types of trees?" "How about human cells? What are the different parts and their functions?" I suggested.

Nick pulled out his science book and started reading aloud. Cody concentrated and was able to repeat everything Nick said word for word.

"You are never going to have to study for tests again. I'm so jealous," Nick commented.

"I never had to study for tests before. Maybe we should swap powers," Cody suggested.

"No way! I don't want to be known as some major brainiac," Nick scoffed.

"Don't worry. You're not," Cody mumbled.

"Hey!" Nick jumped up and started chasing Cody around the junkyard.

"Knock it off, guys!" I yelled after them. "We don't want to get caught." I grabbed Cody's backpack and packed up his books. That was enough testing for the day.

When I caught up to them, Nick was holding Cody over his head and screaming like a Tusken Raider. "Put me down," Cody yelled.

"Why don't you time me to see how long I can hold you up?" Nick yelled back.

"Guys, hush! There's someone coming!" I crouched behind an old desk. Nick dropped Cody and hid next to me. Cody was moaning on the ground.

"Nick!" I whispered loudly.

"Sorry, I panicked," Nick confessed.

I reached over and pulled Cody toward us. He stopped groaning. All of a sudden, we noticed a large, black SUV slowly driving near us. It was one of those cars you see in movies that the "good guys" usually drive. A man wearing a suit and dark sunglasses stepped out. He paused briefly and looked all around. Then he got back in the SUV and drove off. We breathed a sigh of relief.

"Do you think he was looking for us?" Nick asked apprehensively.

"I'm not sure. But let's get out of here," I stated.

We all agreed. We ran as fast as we could to the fence that we'd climbed over. We kept running until the junkyard was far behind us.

We finally arrived at our choice pizza place. Even through the summer, the Friday tradition of pizza and doughnuts carried on. After purchasing our goods, we walked home.

"Who was that guy?" Nick asked.

"I didn't recognize him," Cody said.

"Me either. I wonder if it was because we were using our powers." I checked my watch. The other boys did the same. Cody and I were still in the green. Nick was still down one green mark.

As we were walking, I noticed the same SUV driving toward us. We stopped briefly, and it continued past us. We finally reached Cody's house and enjoyed our pizza. We were debating which video games to play when all of a sudden, there was a crash. We ran out of the room.

Cara, Cody's sister, was lying on the floor with a jump rope next to her. "My foot hurts," Cara yelled.

"Help me get her up," Cody told me.

Cody and I knelt next to her and helped her to stand.

"My foot is all better." Cara looked up at her brother. "What did you do?"

"We didn't do anything. We just helped you up. I'm so glad you aren't hurt," Cody said with a forced smile.

Cara muttered a "Thanks," picked up her jump rope, and kept jumping. We went back to Cody's room and finished our meal.

"You don't think she'll tell anyone?" I asked warily.

"Nah. She's not supposed to jump rope in the house anyway.

If my parents hear she got hurt, they would just take it away," Cody replied calmly.

That appeased me, and we continued to plan our gaming evening.

CHAPTER 8

MR. MALCOLM

"Why does school have to start tomorrow?" Nick asked in anguish.

We were at school getting our schedules and having class pictures taken. Not only did we need to come to school on the last day of summer, we also had to get dressed up for it.

Summer had passed way too quickly. We continued doing tests, trying to expand our powers. We found everyday uses for them without attracting too much attention. For example, anytime Cody's mom asked him to go to the store, she just told him what she needed, and he remembered perfectly. I subtly healed a few more customers who came into the store. Nick had even lifted my desk so I could clear old papers from underneath.

But unfortunately, summer was over, and school was beginning. Cody had no trouble with school starting. He was the one who actually enjoyed school. Since this was our senior year, we would begin looking at colleges to decide what we would do after high school.

"Aw, man, we only have PE together," Nick complained, staring at Cody and my schedules. "You guys have all those AP classes."

"If you had studied in your previous classes, you wouldn't have to retake so many of them," Cody said with an attitude.

Nick crumpled up his schedule and shoved it in his pocket. I kept trying to remind Cody not to make Nick angry. He had a bit of a temper and now he had the power of Strength.

As we all headed off the schoolgrounds, we heard a familiar voice say, "Hey, guys, wait up!" We turned and saw Kelly running toward us. "I just got my schedule. What are you guys taking?"

We compared schedules and found that we wouldn't be sharing any classes with her. "Aw, bummer. I was hoping to do more projects with you guys. Cody, why are you taking so many AP classes?" Kelly asked.

"My parents told me it looks good on college applications."

"Ha! Only if you pass all the AP exams. Good luck studying in the spring," Kelly retorted.

We smiled at each other. If only she knew.

"Kelly, want to join us for video games?" I offered in a friendly way.

"Yeah, we want to make the most of our final day of freedom," Nick announced.

"Sure, thanks," Kelly replied cheerfully.

Kelly was one of the few girls who could keep up with us in video games. She was very skilled at first-person shooters and RPGs. She could even beat us at Smash Brothers.

About fifteen minutes later, we arrived at our cul-de-sac. I stopped dead in my tracks when I saw the black SUV from the junkyard parked right in front of my house.

Kelly noticed my hesitation. "Jay, what's the matter?" At that point, the other boys noticed it.

"You guys start playing, and I'll catch up with you in a bit," I said as I started jogging toward my house.

"Wha—? Is everything all right?" she yelled after me. Nick and Cody kept walking in silence, motioning for her to follow. She seemed bewildered but went along with them.

I opened the front door and heard my mom and a man's voice I didn't recognize. I quietly set down my backpack and walked toward the kitchen.

"Oh, Jay, perfect timing! This is Mr. Malcolm. He was telling me about a job opportunity for you." She gestured toward the man who turned to face me.

It was the same man I saw earlier in the summer at the junkyard, except he wasn't wearing his sunglasses. He was above-average height and had a solid build. Clean-shaven, he seemed like he just returned from the Caribbean.

"Hello, Jay." He held out his hand.

"Hello," I responded, shaking his hand cautiously.

"I was just telling your mother about an internship I'd like to tell you about. You see, I'm a representative from the Power Store. We've been watching you, and we think you have great potential."

"So have you been following my friends and me?" I asked suspiciously.

Mr. Malcolm chuckled. "Just the one time you saw me at the junkyard. I wanted to make sure you were being responsible."

So he was following us.

"Jay, you seem to have taken quite well to your ability. You've been responsible at using it, not attracting attention to yourself, and benefitting others. We'd like for you to consider working with

us at our training center. It would be a few hours each week after school. We're attempting to broaden our market, and hiring a student like you may be a way to get the youth interested."

I nodded in a noncommittal way.

"Think about it, all right? Feel free to invite your friends as well. We have a wonderful facility that allows you to test your powers." Mr. Malcolm handed me a small business card. It simply said, "Mr. Malcolm, Power Store Representative." There was an address and a phone number at the bottom of the card.

"I look forward to hearing from you." Mr. Malcolm stood up and held out his hand to me. I shook it hesitantly, and he walked out the front door.

"Isn't that exciting, Jay? I knew you would be responsible with your power," my mom exclaimed proudly. "You should seriously consider his offer."

"But who is he? And how did he know where to find me?" I demanded.

"Well, they implanted a small tracking device inside you. It's the store's way of making sure that the powers are being used well," she replied calmly, sipping her tea.

"A tracking device?" I looked at my wrist, where the Manager had implanted my power source. "This has been tracking me the whole time? You never told me."

"I'm sorry. I didn't think it would upset you that much. The Manager explained it all to your father and me. After lots of thought, we gave our consent in case you decided to get a full power."

My parents knew I would go back.

"Jay, your father and I have known about this store for years. I know several adults who have powers as well. They all agreed that it was a wonderful idea for you to have a power as well. We trust you with this power, Jay."

Wait, Mom knows other people with powers? Who else? I was even more confused. "All right, so let's say I do accept this job. What about college? Med school?" I was definitely confused.

"Honey, you know that your father and I trust the decisions you make. If you wish to go to med school, we'd love that. We just thought that with the power you chose, you might consider other options. This internship may help you to develop your power and help more people."

"So you'd be all right if I went off to this random place and worked there instead of college?"

"Yes, Jay. Wouldn't it be easier?" she asked honestly.

I reflected for a moment. My parents had wanted me to choose a power and use it. I didn't realize that my whole career plan would become unnecessary in the process.

"Honey, just think about it. Promise?" She looked up at me.

"Okay, Mom. I promise."

"Good. Now where are Nick and Cody?"

I had completely forgotten about them. I gave Mom a quick hug and jogged back to Nick's house. They were in the middle of Star Wars Battlefront when Nick yelled at me, "Dude, what happened?" He paused the game, at which point Cody and Kelly started complaining.

I sat down and held out the business card.

"Who's Mr. Malcolm?" Cody asked, passing the card back to me.

"He's a representative from," I paused a few seconds, "that store."

Nick and Cody glanced at each other and then at Kelly.

"Fine, fine. I'll leave. I can take a hint." She started to stand up.

"No, it's fine. Can you keep a secret?" I asked.

"Sure, what's the secret?" Kelly replied curiously.

Nick stood up next to his bed and picked it up with one hand. He set it down after holding it up for a few seconds.

"Whoa! How did you ... ?" Kelly stammered.

Then, he grabbed Cody's hand and squeezed it. We could hear a few cracks, and then Cody started screaming in pain. Kelly was horrified. I quickly grabbed my friend's hand, and he calmed down.

"What, how did ...? You're ..." Kelly couldn't figure out how to respond.

"Kelly, my parents took me to a store that sells powers for my birthday. I chose the power to Heal. Nick got Strength, and Cody chose Memory. That's why he's taking so many AP classes. He remembers everything that he reads or hears." I gestured to Cody for a demonstration.

"Kelly, this year your classes are biology, calculus, English, French 4, PE, and world history." Cody looked at her for confirmation.

"Come on, man. That's not that impressive," Nick scoffed. "Recite pi."

Nick showed his math book to Kelly as Cody recited the first hundred digits of pi.

"Wow, that's cool." Kelly was slowly processing everything. "So, what's with the business card?"

That was another of Kelly's amazing characteristics. She was comfortable with weird.

"Mr. Malcolm is a representative from the Power Store. He invited all of us to do this internship. He said we would just have to talk about using our powers, and they'd use what we said to attract more clients. There's even a place where we can test our powers," I explained.

"Hmm, sounds interesting," Cody stated, considering what I said.

"Awesome! Let's go sign up." Nick said excitedly.

"I'm not too sure, guys. Did you know that we were implanted with a tracking device?"

"Where? Are you serious?" Nick exclaimed.

"Yeah. It's the way they track how we use our powers," Cody responded calmly.

"You knew?" I was surprised at my friend.

"Of course. The Manager explained it to us. Don't you remember?" Cody replied.

"Dude, we don't all have your memory," Nick said, sighing in irritation.

"Well, what's the harm in checking it out? It sounds like fun," Kelly piped in.

We all looked at her, unsure how to respond. "Oh, come on. I know I don't have a power, but it'd be fun to just observe," Kelly said enthusiastically.

"Okay, fine. We'll try it out after school tomorrow," I replied looking at the address. It was on the same street as the store. We all agreed to meet at the bus stop after school to head right over.

"Well, one plus about this week is that school starts on Wednesday. Only three days until the weekend," Nick exclaimed.

Cody noticed the time and sensibly suggested that we call it quits on video games. We all left Nick's house and walked home. Kelly only lived a few blocks away from our cul-de-sac.

After saying goodbye to everyone, I walked to my house. I felt more assured since my friends would be with me. However, I couldn't quite shake the feeling that something bad was about to happen.

CHAPTER 9

TRAINING CENTER

"Stop it! Please just stop!" Cody yelled at the football team. They decided to start off the school year by picking on their favorite victim. They each took turns taking his books and throwing them down the hall.

Lunch had just started when Nick and I heard Cody's familiar cry. "Hey, back off," Nick said, walking straight up to Brandon, the quarterback.

"Oh, really, short stuff? What are you gonna do about it?" he taunted.

"I'm going to tell you once. Give my friend's books back to him, or you will pay," Nick replied with his fists clenched.

"Ha! Make me." The quarterback leaned down and was right in Nick's face. All of a sudden, *whack*! Nick punched him hard in the nose. Blood gushed down Brandon's face, and he screamed in agony. Unfortunately, Nick did not stop. He grabbed his right arm and twisted it completely behind his back. The other football players didn't know what to do. They ran away, yelling, as did all the other students.

I boldly walked up to Nick and calmly said, "Nick, stop!" Nick looked up with fury in his eyes and realized what was happening. He let go of the football player, who slumped to the floor, writhing in pain. I calmly stepped up to him and put a hand on his shoulder. Soon the blood stopped, and he ceased yelling.

"What? What did you do?" Brandon asked frantically.

"If you ever come near my friends again, worse things will happen to you. And I won't be there to stop it," I said, looking directly in his eyes.

Brandon didn't need to be told twice. He got up and ran in the direction of his teammates. Nick and I had just started picking up Cody's books when we suddenly heard a loud *beep!* Nick looked down at his watch. It only had one green mark left.

"Oh no. I only have one strike left. What happens when the last one is gone?" Nick asked anxiously.

"I'm not sure," Cody confessed.

Having collected all of Cody's books, we walked toward the lunchroom. I thought I saw Ms. James poke her head out of her classroom.

We ate in silence as Kelly sat there, blabbing away about her classes. Finally, we finished our last class of the day. All four of us met at the bus stop and waited for our bus. When it arrived, we got on and sat in the back.

"So what was the fight about?" Kelly asked innocently.

"How did you know about that?" Nick asked defensively.

"Seriously? A fight happens on the first day of school, and you don't think anyone talked about it?"

I briefly told Kelly what happened.

"Aw, why did you heal him? Brandon's a jerk, and he would've deserved it if he lost his throwing arm for the season." Kelly sat back, smiling. I guess she was picturing Brandon as a benchwarmer.

"It was tempting. But healing him was the right thing to do. Just think how angry the coach or his father would've been if he had come home with a broken nose and a broken arm," Cody offered sensibly.

"He would've started asking questions, and they would've blamed us," I added.

"Still, I think you're too generous with your power, Jay. And you, Nick, you need to control your temper. It was bad enough before you got a power." Kelly had witnessed Nick get angry before.

Nick nodded humbly. "I know, but Cody was getting picked on just for being smart."

"Well you never have to worry about that happening to you!" Kelly laughed.

Nick grumbled in response and then turned his head toward the window.

Soon, we reached our destination. It looked like an old, abandoned factory, but maybe that's what they wanted people to think. We walked up to the large, black, iron gate. On the side, we saw an intercom. I pressed the button and said, "Hello?"

A few seconds later, we heard an impatient voice. "Yes, what do you want?"

"Um, we're here because Mr. Malcolm invited us.

"Oh, my apologies. Of course. Come in, come in!" We heard a buzz and the gate swung open. We walked inside and soon were at the entrance to the factory. The doors automatically opened as we approached it.

"Welcome to the Training Center! We're pleased to have you with us," said a man who had earlier spoke with us at the gate.

"I'm the Doorkeeper. I make sure that only those worthy can enter this facility. I trust you had no trouble finding us."

"Nope, none at all," I responded.

"Excellent. We try not to be too obvious to the rest of the population, but not too difficult to find either. Come have a seat."

We all sat on a fluffy white couch. He sat opposite us. "So which powers did you all choose?" he asked us.

"Cody chose Memory, Nick chose Strength, and I chose Heal," I answered.

"I don't have a power. I'm just here to observe," added Kelly.

The man's eyebrows furrowed a bit, but he smiled. "No trouble at all. We don't hide what we do here. Although you do seem worthy of a power, my dear," he said, looking at Kelly.

"I'm still making up my mind," she replied nonchalantly.

"Of course. No rush. Let's have a tour, shall we?" He gestured toward a large hall. It reminded me of a gym with racquetball court–sized rooms on either side. Inside, we saw people of different ages practicing a variety of powers. Each room had a robot inside, who seemed to be conducting their drills.

"We at the Power Store want to make sure that we equip all our clients the best way we can. Many who gain powers choose to come and work here. They sometimes find it difficult to be a part of the general population," the Doorkeeper explained.

We came to an empty room, at which point the Doorkeeper stopped. "Who would like to try his power with a training-bot?" he asked.

"I will," Nick volunteered. He entered the room and saw his training-bot. The bot was about three feet tall and covered in shiny metal.

"Please state your name and your power," the bot said in a computerized voice.

"I'm Nick, and I have Strength."

The bot said, "Pick me up."

Nick looked back at us to check that we were watching. We gave him a thumbs-up, and he walked toward the bot. He reached out with one arm, but the bot didn't even budge. Nick grabbed it with both arms and struggled with all his might.

After a few seconds, the bot said, "During your training, I will teach you how to use your power properly until you have unlimited strength. Stand with your feet a shoulder-width apart, bend your legs, and lift."

Nick tried again. Slowly, he was able to lift the bot one or two inches off the ground. He suddenly dropped the bot and collapsed on the floor.

"Congratulations, Nick. You just picked up ten tons. With more training, you will be able to pick up anything."

"Impressive," the Doorkeeper muttered. "Most impressive."

Nick continued his training, while Kelly, Cody, and I continued the tour. "You see, each bot is programmed to adequately challenge each power."

"So what would it do for me?" Cody asked.

The Doorkeeper gestured to the next unoccupied room. Cody entered and stated his name and power to the bot. The bot started reciting the dictionary. It stopped after a minute. Cody accurately recited everything.

"That's incredible," Kelly exclaimed. "He would win so much money on *Jeopardy!*"

"No, no, no. Remember, these powers can only be used to benefit others, not for selfish gain," the Doorkeeper warned.

"Sir, Nick's watch already lost two green bars. What happens if he loses his final one?" I asked anxiously.

"Oh, no need to worry about that. Nobody has ever lost all three."

He hurried us along to another room. This room was filled with people lying on hospital beds. "Well, Jay, would you like to test your ability?"

"Who are all these people?" I was shocked to see dozens of gurneys.

"Many people, once they have powers, choose to live here. We don't actually have any healers on staff right now. I'm sure Mr. Malcolm thought you would be perfect for this job."

"How did they get hurt?"

"Not all train with bots. Sometimes they train using each other. Obviously, this is all on a volunteer basis. But people do get injured."

Kelly and I hurried to the door and entered. I instantly started grabbing people's hands. One by one, they got up, stretched, and left as if nothing had ever happened. I healed everyone before I noticed how tired I was. I quickly put my hand on my chest and healed myself.

"You need to be careful, Jay, not to expend your power so quickly," the Doorkeeper warned.

"I don't get it, though. It was as if they expected me."

The Doorkeeper nodded. "Let me show you one more room, Jay." He walked outside and waited for us to follow.

He took us through a large black door, and we saw a screen that covered an entire wall. It was a map of the United States. On it were several hundred small green dots, either moving or staying still.

"What is this?" Kelly asked, staring at a dot. She touched one of the green dots and a smaller screen popped up.

The screen showed a picture of a woman in her forties. Underneath the picture it said, "Jamie Carl, Control."

"These are all the people to whom we have given powers," the Doorkeeper responded proudly. "Here you are, Jay." He zoomed in on an area with an extremely high concentration of dots. He selected one, and up popped my picture. Next to the photo, it said, "Jay Holden, Heal."

"So this is what the tracking device does," I stated.

"Exactly. We monitor all power activity and all power users." He zoomed the map out and continued. "This tracking device also allows us to do a search on powers and people. For example, let's see how many have the power to Heal."

He typed the word "Heal" into the search. About twenty dots showed up all over the country.

"Wow," I responded. "There aren't many healers."

"The most popular powers seem to be Strength, Flight, and Control. Here are the four stores we have currently. You can tell by the high concentration of powers. This is the only training facility in the country," he explained.

"So what now? We come here to train?" I asked.

"If you choose to. We welcome people with powers to come here for as long as they like. We encourage all people to train until they feel comfortable with their powers. After that, it's their choice to stay or continue in the world." The Doorkeeper led us back through the hallway.

As we passed Cody's room, we could hear him reciting all the names of the Roman emperors and the years they reigned. I knocked on the door, and Cody turned around.

"Jay, this has been so amazing. I memorized *War and Peace*," Cody exclaimed proudly. He looked like he was about to pass out.

"Good job, man. I think we're done for the day." I reached out my hand to Cody, who instantly looked better. "Come on. Let's go get Nick."

We continued to walk down the hall and heard Nick yelling loudly in frustration. The bot was almost half a foot off the floor. He let it go and again fell to the ground in exhaustion. I ran in and helped him up.

"Congratulations. You held up ten tons for fifteen seconds."

"Phew! Now *that* was a good workout." Nick stretched a bit and then walked out with me.

"Remember, you all are welcome at any time. Now, young lady, while we are open for outsiders, we prefer that all participants have a power."

"All right, all right," Kelly replied in surrender. "I'll go get a power."

"Excellent choice. The Manager should still be there. We'll see you soon!" He waved us out the door, which closed behind us, and we walked toward the Power Store.

"That was awesome!" Nick shouted.

"That was so much fun," Cody continued.

"That was interesting," I offered.

"That was freaky," Kelly yelled. "You guys are serious about this?"

"Yeah. What's the problem? Come on, let's go get you a power," I replied.

"No way! I'd rather not be turned into some freak who's a dot on a screen, thank you very much," Kelly countered.

"What screen?" Cody asked.

"We saw a screen that showed everyone with powers," I explained.

"Even us?" Cody wondered.

"I guess so. I saw a picture of me with my name and my power listed."

"Oh, who cares?" Nick exclaimed. "This is seriously one of the greatest things that has ever happened! We actually get to go to a place where we can practice our powers!" He was exultant.

Cody and I nodded our consent, while Kelly just shook her head. "You guys are weird," she said and waved dismissively.

Kelly could not be persuaded to get a power. So we headed to the bus stop, waited a few minutes, and got on our bus. About twenty minutes later, we were back on our street. The sun had almost completely set, and we went off in our separate directions.

CHAPTER 10

POWERS OR SCHOOL?

"Son, you've gotten home late every night this week." My mom was concerned. A few weeks had passed, and we had gone to the training center almost every day.

"Are you boys getting in trouble?" my dad asked me sternly.

"No, we've been working at the training center," I explained.

"Really? Why didn't you tell me before?" Mom asked.

"Training center? At the hospital?" Dad looked at me.

"No, Dad. It's with the Power Store. There's a training center near the store, and we've been practicing our powers."

"That's excellent, son. Are you making enough time for your homework?" he continued.

"Yeah, we don't go every day. We sometimes study at Cody's house." That wasn't entirely true, but I wasn't too worried about my grades.

"Just remember, school comes first," Dad instructed.

"Of course, Dad." I nodded and continued eating my dinner.

I had started to consider whether I needed to go to school. I had the power to Heal. Why would I need to become a surgeon to help people? I was already doing a great job now. But I didn't want to tell my parents that just yet.

After washing dishes, I retreated to my room and opened my biology book. I had been reading the same chapter for the last few days and could not make sense of it. I had started to feel bitter about signing up for the class. Anyway, I could just ask Cody to do my homework for me. *He* never needed to study.

I slammed my book shut and continued on to other work. I had an essay due the next day on a book I was supposed to have read. I had neglected that too. I did a quick search online for an abridged version. I then scanned the first few lines of each chapter and halfheartedly typed my paper. After printing it and stashing it in my backpack, I promptly fell asleep.

The next day, it seemed like there was a cloud over my head. Nothing seemed to go my way. I bombed the quiz in biology and could not stay awake in statistics. Mr. Nan was droning on about some equation that I already knew, and I didn't feel the need to participate.

By the time I got to English, I was in a bad mood. Ms. James collected all our papers as we read silently. After ten minutes, she had us pair up and create a compare/contrast chart using two characters from the book. My partner, Neil, obviously hadn't read the book either. By the end of the class, we only had one point in each column. As I was leaving, I heard Ms. James call out, "Jay, may I see you for a minute?"

I slowly turned around and trudged up to her desk. She held up my paper. "You didn't put much effort into this."

I shook my head, admitting my guilt.

Ms. James sighed. "What's wrong, Jay? At the end of last year, you had a wonderful goal lined up. You knew what you were going to do, and now it seems that you've lost your way." She sounded genuinely concerned for me.

"Maybe I have a different goal," I responded a bit haughtily.

"What might that be?" she asked, ignoring my attitude.

I shrugged and put my head down.

"Jay, you're smarter than this. You can do work that most of your classmates wouldn't be able to if they wanted. Why are you giving this up?"

"I found something better," I answered harshly.

Ms. James sat back in her chair. "Are you going to drop out of school, Jay? You know that a high school diploma is the bare minimum for getting anywhere in life."

"Not everywhere."

Ms. James sighed. "Well, I hope you find a new goal soon. If you want, I'll allow you a week to redo your paper. That'll show me what you have decided." She handed me my paper, and I grabbed it quickly. I hadn't noticed it before, but she had a watch on her wrist. It was the same as … I looked up at her quickly, and she seemed not to notice. I slowly walked out of the classroom, stunned.

By the time I reached PE, my friends were already in their PE clothes and motioning me to hurry up. I made it onto my number just before Mr. Deway blew the tardy whistle. Today was another running day. Since we were seniors, Mr. Deway required us to run two miles. Nick, Cody, and I didn't mind this. They knew I could just heal them. We all got behind the line and started running after our teacher blew the whistle.

We had been fast before, but with my power, we sprinted the whole way. Every minute or so, I held out my hand to my friends, and they were instantly reenergized. We couldn't run too fast or we would draw attention to ourselves. But we were still able to

finish in just over thirteen minutes. We huffed and puffed out to the basketball courts. When our teacher was preoccupied with the rest of the class, I motioned them over.

After healing them, I whispered, "Ms. James has a watch!"

My two friends looked at me curiously.

"Of course she does. She's a teacher," Nick remarked.

"No, I mean one of these!" I held up my watch with my power meter. They looked surprised.

"Really? Are you sure?" Cody asked warily.

"Dude, it was the same watch as we have. She has a power." Nick and Cody shushed me. Some other students had finished running and were starting to join us on the court.

"We'll talk more later," I remarked. Cody and Nick nodded and kept shooting baskets.

Half an hour later, the bell rang. The afternoon dragged on. I could not wait to keep talking to my friends. I still had another twenty-five minutes in US history. I was so impatient to be done with school that I almost didn't notice the watch on my teacher's wrist. I rubbed my eyes and looked again. My history teacher, Mr. Lambert, was wearing a watch just like mine. I started thinking about my other teachers. *Did they all have powers?*

The bell rang, and I went off to my last class. In Spanish, the teacher was lecturing about irregular past tense verbs. I could not take my focus off my Spanish teacher's watch. *She had a watch too.*

I could not wait to tell my friends. When the final bell rang, I ran out of class toward our meeting place. Cody came running, as well as Nick.

"They all have powers," we all shouted at once.

"Really? Hold on. One at a time," Cody said, taking control of the group.

"Mr. Lambert and Mrs. Rodriguez have watches," I started.

"I saw Mrs. Rodriguez' watch too. And Mr. White has one," Nick continued.

"I saw Ms. James's watch, and Mr. Rousseau has one too," Cody finished.

"Do all our teachers have powers?" Nick asked.

"Yes, yes we do!" We all jumped and turned to see Ms. James standing right behind us. "Gentlemen, let's have a chat in my classroom." Ms. James turned, expecting us to follow.

"Now we're in for it," Nick admitted. Cody and I weren't sure what to think.

We reached Ms. James's classroom and sat in the "lounge." It had a few comfy couches surrounding the class library. It was decorated with random items and posters from Ms. James's life. She even had a framed and signed picture of George Lucas. She was very proud of it.

We all sat down and waited for Ms. James to start.

"So, gentlemen, you got your powers, and you've probably found the training center. You may have even started thinking that you don't need school anymore. Am I right?" We all nodded sheepishly. "Here's the thing. It is my job to ensure that each of you graduates from high school. Any student of mine who fails means I lose a green mark." She showed us her watch, which still showed three glowing marks. "I want your solemn promise that none of you will fail my class. If you do, I will be in debt." She glared solemnly at each of us.

"What is debt?" Cody asked curiously.

Ms. James sighed. "You don't want to know," she replied as if speaking from experience.

"But I already have two strikes!" Nick showed Ms. James his watch.

Ms. James looked concerned. "I'm sorry about that, Nick. You'll just have to be really careful with your power. No more public demonstrations. Keep going to the training center. It will help you to control your power and learn how to use it in public."

"Ms. James," I said cautiously, "what's your power?"

Ms. James smiled. "Now that is a personal question, Jay. How about if I give you three guesses? If you get it right, I'll tell you."

I reflected over my time in Ms. James's classes. I thought about how the students behaved and what she enjoyed. I tried to think of her little teaching quirks that helped us remember our grammar or vocabulary words.

"Is Calm your power?" I asked, looking up at her.

"Yes, it is. Very perceptive, Jay. I can keep people and situations around me calm. Unfortunately, the dark side of my power is to remove calmness. I could turn a peaceful and loving school into a horrific scene of chaos. But, of course, I choose not to."

"I'm sorry that I didn't do well on the paper. I'll try harder and have it done by next week," I promised.

"That's good, Jay. I will not have any of you dropping out of high school for a full-time job at the training center." Ms. James stood up and gestured us toward the door. "I'll see you all tomorrow," she said, closing the door behind us.

We were unsure what to do. We wanted to go to the training center, but we also didn't want Ms. James to have any strikes. We decided to do the right thing: walk home and complete our homework.

CHAPTER 11

THE DEMONSTRATION

"Man, it's almost break," Nick yelled triumphantly. The three of us were walking toward the gas station for "Thirsty Thursdays."

The school year had continued uneventfully, and next week would be spring break. The warning from Ms. James had really sunk in. We decided we would only go to the training center on the weekends, and only then if we had our homework finished. Cody had no trouble with this. He had already read through all the textbooks for his four AP classes. Nick was struggling even with his regular classes. However, his difficulty mostly came from the fact that he did not want to complete school.

"Why does it even matter?" he demanded. "We're all just going to go to work at the training center. Why do we even need school?"

I was doing pretty well. Cody had been helping me study, and I was slowly beginning to understand the advanced concepts in AP biology. Ms. James had continued to encourage all three of us to keep studying and do our best.

We got our drinks and started home, discussing what we were going to do that week.

"I say we go to the training center every day! Maybe they'll even let us stay at night," Nick suggested.

"Nick, do you really want to stay with all those other people?" Cody asked.

"Xander doesn't seem that bad," Nick replied defensively.

"Yeah, but I wouldn't want to end up like him," Cody admitted.

Xander was one of the people we had met in the training center. He was in his mid-twenties and had been living at the training center since he finished high school. He seemed perfectly content to just live there. He never really spoke about his family, and we didn't want to pry. He had the power of Flight and spent most of his days training with bots with built-in lasers. He was also one of the people I healed the first time we went there.

We agreed to take our drinks with us to the training center. We got on the bus and rode in silence. Cody had another book of Shakespeare's poems that he was memorizing. I just looked out the window, wondering about Nick. There were a few times in the past month that he had almost lost it at school. Thankfully, Cody and I were there to calm him down. Still, it was unnerving.

When we arrived, the gate had already swung open, and the Doorkeeper was there to greet us. "Welcome, boys! It's wonderful to see you again. We have a special guest today and will be doing a demonstration for him," he said as he walked down the hall, motioning us to follow.

"A demonstration?" Cody asked. "Isn't that against the rules?"

"Oh, goodness no! That rule only applies to outsiders. We all have powers here, so there's nothing to be worried about."

He opened a door and we entered. We were in a huge gym with a large open space in the middle. We saw several hundred people, some of whom we recognized. We saw Xander and walked over to him.

"Hey, high-schoolers! We're performing for the bigwig today," Xander explained excitedly.

"Who?" I asked.

Xander pointed to the top of one of the walls. It looked like it was a sort of dark-glass-covered patio built into the gym. He gestured toward a silhouette of a man, but we couldn't make out who it was.

"That's the big boss! He's the one we'll be demonstrating for."

"But who is he? Is he the Manager?" Cody asked.

"Nah, man. He's the Owner. He's the one who figured out how to create these powers. He's the lead scientist, and he's come to check on our progress. He is the man that you have to thank for all of this!" He gestured all around him.

Tap, tap, tap.

"Ahem!" The Doorkeeper was holding a microphone and standing in the middle of the room. "May I have your attention please? This is a very wonderful day for all of us. We have a special guest to witness our demonstration. Please give a big hand for the Owner!" He gestured toward the silhouette and applauded. Everyone else started applauding and cheering as well. The silhouette seemed to wave back.

"Now, we will call up individuals one at a time to demonstrate their skills with a bot. They will have approximately fifteen seconds to show us what they can do. Gabe Alcut, you are up first."

Gabe was about Cody's height, but he looked much older. He stood in the center of the gym. His bot was next to him, and he directed his hand toward it. Suddenly, the metal on the bot melted and fell in a pile of goo on the floor. Everyone clapped as Gabe bowed and walked off.

A few minutes later, Xander was called up. He stood in the ready position. The bot took aim and fired a laser bolt at Xander. He was already ten feet in the air before the bolt reached him. Xander continued to skillfully and easily dodge all the bot's laser bolts. Soon, his time was done, and we all cheered for him.

I noticed that someone had been hit by one of the bolts. His arm had a hole in it the size of a quarter. The man was trying to hold himself together, but it was obvious he was in pain. I reached out and touched his arm. Flesh soon filled up the hole, and he was healed.

He looked down at me and offered me his hand. "Thank you, young man. You have a true gift. My name is Ben. If you ever need anything, just holler. I'll hear you."

"It's my pleasure, Ben. I'm Jay."

"I won't forget that," Ben replied solemnly.

I kept walking around the facility, half looking for any of my teachers.

"Gina James," the Doorkeeper yelled.

I froze.

Our English teacher is here. I thought as I turned to face the crowd. My teacher calmly walked into the center of the gym. I soon heard people complaining and yelling. It seemed that they were going to start a riot. Just as quickly as that happened, everyone quieted and calmed down. Everyone stared at each other inquisitively. Then they realized that Ms. James was the one who caused them to go crazy. They wildly applauded her. She simply smiled, bowed, and rejoined the crowd.

"Cody Clay," the Doorkeeper continued.

Cody boldly stepped out. He seemed to have created a plan. "I would like for everyone to shout their names all at once. Now!" Cody announced.

There was a loud shout of random names. Cody paused briefly and then flawlessly and accurately named the twenty-seven people who were closest to him. There was huge applause as he rejoined Nick and me.

"Nick Carr."

Nick walked up to where the bot stood. He calmly picked it up and held it over his head. "One ton," spoke the bot. "Two tons. Three tons. Four tons." The bot kept increasing every second. Nick didn't seem to notice the weight was increasing. When the bot reached ten tons, nobody moved. Nick just stood there, holding the bot above his head, his arms not even shaking.

After fifteen seconds, Nick calmly put the bot down. The room exploded in cheers and applause. Everyone was amazed at Nick's strength. Even the Doorkeeper applauded.

Nick seemed to sway as he walked over to me. I grabbed him, and Nick instantly felt fine. The Doorkeeper approached Nick and said, "Well done, Nick. The Owner would like to speak to you." A bot standing at attention next to the Doorkeeper appeared ready to lead Nick to the Owner. Nick gave us an unsure look, but we encouraged him on. He slowly followed the bot and walked through a door, leaving everyone else behind.

"Wonderful job, everyone! We have one more person I'd like to introduce. You may recognize Jay. He's been spending a lot of time in the infirmary, making sure we all stay healthy." Everyone who had been in the infirmary in the last several months recognized me. They gave me a warm round of applause. I just politely waved at everyone.

"Thank you for your participation. Continue with your training exercises, please!" And with that, the demonstration was over. Everyone slowly headed their separate ways and returned to training.

"Wasn't that awesome? I never knew that all these people had different powers," Cody exclaimed.

"That was so cool what you did. I didn't know you could listen to multiple things at once," I complimented my friend.

Cody smiled smugly and said, "I wonder what's going on with Nick."

At that moment, we noticed Nick approaching us, his face gleaming.

"What happened?" Cody asked excitedly.

"I met the Owner! He's a really cool guy and seemed super chill," Nick responded.

"What did he want?" I continued the questioning.

"He told me he liked how well I used my power," Nick answered with pride.

"Does he know you have two strikes?" Cody asked, reminding Nick.

"Oh, he didn't care about that. He just liked my performance and wanted to tell me himself."

"Well, good for you. I don't think he did that with anyone else," I commented. "Let's head back home." I headed toward the door with Cody. Nick couldn't decide if he wanted to leave or stay.

"Leaving so soon, Nick?" the Doorkeeper asked.

"Uh, yeah. I have school tomorrow," Nick responded sheepishly.

"Well, remember the Owner's offer," the Doorkeeper stated as if sharing a secret.

"Come on, Nick!" Cody shouted from the door.

"I'm coming," he responded, still looking toward the gym. He waved to the Doorkeeper and joined us. We were discussing the different powers we saw.

"Can you imagine being able to fly?" Cody exclaimed.

"I know! Xander chose an awesome power," I responded.

We were so engrossed in our conversation that we didn't even notice how quiet Nick was. We sat at the bus stop and kept talking. Finally, our bus arrived. Cody and I were about to get on when I called to Nick, "Are you coming, Nick?"

"Huh?" Nick was unaware of what was going on. "Oh yeah." Nick followed us on the bus. He didn't say another word the entire way home.

CHAPTER 12

DITCHING SCHOOL

We spent most of our spring break at the training center. There were no more demonstrations, but we started interacting with the other people. The majority of them were in their twenties, with a few a bit older. We didn't see Ms. James or of our teachers, but we didn't expect to.

Sadly, Sunday night approached, and we were in an unhappy mood. One might say that senioritis had fully kicked in, but it was more than that. We started to feel that we belonged at the training center rather than at school. We didn't enjoy mingling with "others" as we called our "nonpower" peers. We couldn't understand how our teachers could have these powers and still want to be with everyone else.

"I don't wanna go back to school," Nick shouted abruptly. He had been in a particularly foul mood since we started walking toward school Monday morning. We had seen it in him before, but today he was out of control.

"Come on, Nick. We only have two months left. We need our high school diplomas, and then we'll be able to live at the training center full time," Cody explained calmly.

"Really, Mr. Smarty? Is that in the rule book for the training center? All who enter must have a high school diploma?" Nick yelled in Cody's face.

"Dude, Nick. Calm down! We're almost at school. Just chill." I was worried about my friend.

Nick walked off in a huff. Cody and I exchanged looks. "What's the matter with him?" I asked.

"Who knows? Maybe his power is getting to his head," Cody offered.

We approached the school and headed to our first class.

The school day passed as usual, taking quizzes and notes, and trying not to get called on by the teacher.

As I was walking out of English, Ms. James stopped me and asked, "Have you seen Nick today?"

I was confused. "Yeah, we walked to school together."

"Hmm, he didn't show up for class." Ms. James was concerned.

"We'll probably see him at lunch."

When I saw Cody at lunch, I said, "Ms. James said that Nick wasn't in class."

"Weird. Where do you think he is?" Cody asked, getting out his water bottle.

"I don't know. He's never just ditched before." We were sitting by ourselves, so no one could hear us.

"Nick didn't seem happy this morning," Cody offered.

"He's not a morning person. But he's never snapped at you like that," I responded, taking a bite of my sandwich.

"Maybe Kelly's seen him." Cody waved at Kelly, who was walking toward us.

"Hey guys! How's saving the world?" Kelly laughed at her own joke.

Cody ignored her comment. "Have you seen Nick today?"

"Nope. Isn't he usually with you two?" Kelly asked with a mouthful of food.

"Yeah, he was really moody this morning," I confessed.

"Have you checked the training center?" Kelly tossed a flaming hot Cheeto into her mouth.

"Oh, shoot. I wonder if he ditched to go train," Cody suggested.

"Well, there you go. He obviously isn't interested in school anymore," Kelly continued.

We sat thoughtfully as Kelly rambled on. The bell rang, and Cody and I headed to PE. At the end of class, I went to US history. I noticed song lyrics written on the whiteboard. As the bell rang, Mr. Lambert stood at his podium. He acted as if we were his choir, and he conducted us through the song.

"Seven more weeks," he sang.

"Seven more weeks," we repeated.

"And we'll be through," Mr. Lambert continued.

"And we'll be through."

"I'll be glad."

"I'll be glad."

"And so will you!"

"And so will you!"

Mr. Lambert led us through this song every Monday. It was his way of getting us excited for the end of the school year. Then he began his lecture on the Great Depression, showing us pictures of bread lines, the Dust Bowl, and "Hoovervilles."

I had never noticed before, but Mr. Lambert had a way of always making history come to life. He obviously wasn't that old, but he spoke about these events as if he had lived through them. Throughout his lecture, he paused to cough and cover his mouth with a handkerchief. He then picked up where he left off.

As students left at the end of class, I slowly approached Mr. Lambert's desk.

"Hello, Jay. What can I do for you?" Mr. Lambert looked at me inquisitively.

I reached out my hand as if to shake his. Mr. Lambert seemed curious but shook my hand back. Mr. Lambert's cough stopped completely.

"A healer! Well thank you very much, Jay. I should've guessed that's the one you would pick," Mr. Lambert said.

"You knew?"

"Of course. These watches aren't exactly sold at SaveMart," Mr. Lambert responded as if it were obvious.

"Would you mind telling me what your power is?" I asked hesitantly.

Mr. Lambert studied me. "I suppose there's no harm since I know yours. Mine is Interesting." He stopped as if that explained everything.

"So what is it?" I asked, staring at my teacher.

"That's my power, Jay. It's called Interesting. I can cause people to become interested or to lose interest in a subject. You may have noticed that students do not get bored in my class. I make them interested in learning history. Now that obviously gives me the responsibility of making it interesting, but it definitely helps."

I reflected over the two years that I had Mr. Lambert as a teacher. I could not remember even one time that I was bored in his class. I smiled. "You made a good choice."

"Thank you kindly. I think you did too," Mr. Lambert admitted.

I walked toward Spanish with a new respect for all my teachers. They were perfect examples of people who used their powers for good. It was inspiring to know that it was possible. Perhaps I *could* find a job where I could use my healing power in a subtle way.

My thoughts drifted to Nick. I hoped he hadn't gone too far. It was comforting to think that he had just gone to the training center.

In Spanish class, we took turns speaking and translating. It occurred to me that Mrs. Rodriguez taught all four levels of Spanish and two levels of French. I wondered if that had something to do with her power.

When school finally ended, I walked off to find Cody. After I found him, we headed toward the bus stop, hoping we would find Nick at the training center.

Thirty minutes later, we were walking through the door. "Good afternoon, Jay and Cody," the Doorkeeper greeted us.

"Have you seen Nick today?" I asked.

"He came by this morning. We were surprised to see him so early, but he said he wanted to train more. He's in the fifth room on the right."

Cody and I jogged in the direction that the Doorkeeper pointed. Inside the fifth room we saw Nick. He looked like he had been working all day. He was having trouble holding the bot. He dropped it and crumpled to the floor, exhausted.

We entered the room and ran over to him. I rested my hand on Nick's chest. His ragged breathing soon returned to normal. He opened his eyes and saw us.

"Hey, guys. Glad you could join me," Nick said casually.

We helped him to his feet and stared at him accusingly. "What?

I didn't feel like going to school today." Nick seemed not to notice how angry we were.

"You ditched us because you didn't *feel like* going to school?" Cody replied angrily.

"Hey, man, watch it," Nick responded nonchalantly. "I'm fine here."

"That's uncool, Nick. We were worried about you," I retorted.

"Look, I don't need school anymore. So why don't you run along, and let me get back to my training?" Nick waved at us dismissively and turned to pick up his bot.

"Come on, Nick. You're not thinking clearly," I pleaded.

"Oh, really?" Nick shot back. "You're out there pretending to be a 'normal,' while I'm in here working my heart out to improve my power." Nick stood right in my face.

"You need to come to school. You have to graduate. Or we'll tell the principal exactly why you weren't at school today." I played my trump card.

Nick took half a step back. "You wouldn't," Nick said, half-convinced.

"Yes, I would. He already knows the teachers have powers. He probably has a power himself. We'll tell him everything," I threatened.

Nick sighed in frustration. Finally he agreed. "Fine. I'll come to school. Don't expect me to be happy about it."

You're never happy about it, I thought, but I decided it would be best not to say it out loud.

"Now would you mind leaving me to train?" He gave us a glance as he prepared to pick up his bot. Cody and I quietly left him to his workout.

"What was all that about?" Cody asked me.

"I don't know. I wonder what else the Owner said to him," I replied pensively.

Cody went to a training room, while I went to the infirmary for the next few hours. Soon, it was time to return home. We got Nick, who was grumbling about having to leave so soon. We got on the bus and had a quiet ride home.

CHAPTER 13

THIRD STRIKE

Nick was true to his word. Every morning, he came to meet Cody and me for school. He always had an unpleasant scowl on his face. It took a while for him to start talking with us again.

School continued without too many troubles. The next major thing we had to think about was AP exams. Cody didn't worry too much. He hadn't needed to study or look over notes—he didn't take notes unless his teachers forced him to—since he got his power. In all our spare time, Cody helped me study as Nick went off alone to the training center.

When exam week arrived, Nick continued with his normal schedule, while Cody and I went to the library to take the exams. I was able to remember most of what Cody and I had studied. Cody finished the exam in less than an hour! The proctors were unsure how to react to Cody, but he seemed confident about his test.

Finally, it was Friday morning, and there were only three weeks left of school. Everyone was happily talking about the prom, graduation, and college plans. The only thing Nick could think about was what he would do after graduation.

"I'll finally be done with this place," Nick exclaimed loudly as we walked through the lunch line. Every once in a while, we'd splurge and buy cafeteria food.

"Oh, come on. It hasn't been that bad," Cody responded.

"Of course you would say that. You were already Mr. Smarty before you got your dumb power," Nick exploded.

"Whoa, why do you have to be so nasty?" I asked in Cody's defense.

"You guys have had your heads in the sand. We don't belong here anymore. Can you believe all these idiots talking about prom? Who cares? Nobody's gonna remember it anyway."

As we headed toward a table with our food, someone accidently bumped into Nick, knocking all the food off his tray. "Oh, I'm so sorry," the student apologized.

"You shouldn't have done that." Nick glared at him, grabbed his arm, and threw him across the room. He flew into the wall and landed in a heap on the floor. Everyone gasped and stared at Nick.

"I've had it with you people! I'm moving on to bigger and better things." There was a loud beep. Nick looked at his watch, which was now completely red. Nick ran out the door, and nobody stopped him.

The principal, Mr. Morgan, was standing in the doorway. He announced, "Everyone continue to eat your lunches." Soon the chatter of the cafeteria resumed as if Nick's outburst never happened.

Cody and I ran toward the injured student and helped him up. He looked at us, astonished. Soon, the principal was standing next to us.

"Have a good day, young man." The principal gazed at the student who simply nodded and walked off.

"Come with me." He turned and walked toward his office. Cody and I struggled to keep up.

We had never been in the principal's office before, and we were unsure as to what would happen next. He sat in a large leather chair behind his desk. Cody and I sat down quietly across from him.

"Nick seems to think he has outgrown school. Unfortunately, he's not the first student who has reacted this way." He continued talking, not paying any attention to our puzzled looks. "My concern is the safety of my students. If Nick doesn't want to be here, you shouldn't force him. I will inform his teachers that he has withdrawn and will not be continuing here. My next concern is you two. Will you both be able to graduate?"

Cody and I were confused.

"Of course, sir. It's important to get at least a high school diploma," I responded.

"I plan to get my doctorate," Cody stated.

Mr. Morgan nodded. "Wonderful. Your power is an excellent aid for that." He smiled knowingly at Cody.

"You know?" Cody asked.

"Of course, Cody. The same way I know that Jay is a healer. It's my job to know which powers my students have. There have been several before you. You may also have figured out that all the teachers have powers." Mr. Morgan showed us his watch.

"So we're not in trouble?" Cody asked.

"No, no. I'm just making sure you'll both be able to graduate. I'm afraid there's not much we can do for Nick. Just continue to be his friends."

"Mr. Morgan, that was his third strike. What's going to happen to him?" I was really concerned.

Mr. Morgan leaned back in his chair. "I'm not sure, Jay. I have never come across anyone who had three strikes. We'll just hope for the best and see what happens." He stood up as if concluding their meeting. So Cody and I walked out of his office.

"That was weird," I confessed.

"I'm starting to get worried about Nick. Even the principal doesn't know what will happen to him," Cody said anxiously.

With lunch over, we trudged off to fifth period. School dragged on that afternoon because we both were anxious to find Nick. After school, we headed off to the training center.

We approached the Doorkeeper and asked, "Have you seen Nick today?"

The Doorkeeper looked surprised. "No, boys. I'm afraid I haven't. Let's check the map, shall we?"

He walked down the hall with us following closely after. The Doorkeeper opened the door and walked to the screen. He grabbed a remote keyboard from the desk and typed in "Nick Carr." We waited a few seconds and then nothing. The Doorkeeper typed in "Nick," and about forty names and faces popped up. None of them were our friend.

"Hmm, that's odd. But we have been having trouble keeping track of our newest clients," the Doorkeeper explained.

"Doorkeeper," Cody said hesitantly, "he used up his third green mark. Does that have anything to do with it?"

"Green mark? What do you mean?"

We indicated our watches. "Oh, those silly things? You shouldn't take those too seriously. Look at my watch!" The Doorkeeper showed us his watch. It was completely red as well. "Don't worry, boys. Nick will show up one of these days. He's always here!"

The Doorkeeper left the screen room and we followed. We were a little wary of his flippant attitude.

We decided to ask someone else who could help us. We walked across the parking lot to the Power Store.

CHAPTER 14

WHO'S NICK?

"Welcome back, boys! I see you've just returned from the training center. Enjoying your powers?" the Manager asked cheerfully.

"Well, there's actually a small problem. One of our friends is missing, and we can't even find him on the tracker," I explained.

"Oh, dear. Well let's check the one here. Nick, right? What is his last name?"

"Carr," I answered.

The Manager typed "Nick Carr" into his tracker, but again nothing came up.

"That's odd. You know, I've been noticing that happening for the past several years. Every once in a while, people seem to fall off the grid." The Manager seemed concerned.

Just then we heard the door open. Mr. Malcolm, the SUV driver, entered the store. "Ah, excuse me, boys." The Manager scurried out of his office and greeted Mr. Malcolm. They conversed in hushed tones until the Manager turned to face us.

"I'm so sorry, boys. Mr. Malcolm needs to meet with me right now. Perhaps you could come back later?" He shooed us out the door and turned the sign to "Closed."

"What do you think is going on?" Cody asked suspiciously.

"I'm not sure," I confessed. "But we definitely need to come back. Let's try to find Nick."

We rode our bus home and walked over to Nick's house. We tried to open the front door, but it was locked.

That's strange. Nick's door is never locked. I knocked, and someone opened the door.

"Yes, who are you? What do you want?" It was Nick's mother.

"Hello, Mrs. Carr. It's Jay and Cody. Is Nick home?" I asked.

"Nick, who is Nick?" Mrs. Carr responded. "Who are you? Why are you bothering me?"

"Mrs. Carr, this isn't funny. We've been Nick's friends since grade school. Where is he? We're worried about him." I demanded.

"I don't know who Nick is, and I don't know who you are. Now get off my property, or I'll call the police." She slammed the door, and I could hear her turn the lock.

We were stunned. Nick's mother didn't know who he was? She didn't know who we were? What was going on?

We ran across the street to Cody's house and barged in. "Mom! Where are you?" Cody yelled.

"I'm right here. What's the matter?" She seemed worried.

"Mom, we can't find Nick," Cody said.

"Nick? Is that a new friend from one of your classes?" she asked innocently.

"Mrs. Clay, do you remember me?" I asked cautiously.

"Jay, of course I know you. You've been Cody's only friend ever since we moved here. Now why don't you both wash up? Dinner will be ready soon. Jay, would you like to stay?"

"Uh, no thank you. I have to go home." I turned and ran out the door to my house as quickly as I could.

I opened the door and frantically yelled, "Mom!"

"In the sewing room."

"Mom, something really weird is happening. Nick is missing, and nobody knows who he is."

"Nick? Who is Nick?" my mom asked honestly.

"Mom, come on. Who have been my best friends forever?"

"Cody, obviously. There is one other person you've mentioned. Oh, what was her name?" She stopped to think. "Kelly! They're the only ones you've brought to the house." She continued working on her sewing project.

What is going on?

I ran to the hall and opened a closet. I found a box of old pictures and dug through it. I found five pictures of Cody, Nick, and I. Except something was wrong. In all five pictures, there was an empty space where Nick should have been standing. There was even a picture of us at one of Nick's birthdays. But he wasn't there. Did he just get erased?

I went to my bedroom, where I had a small box filled with treasures. Nick had given me an original LEGO X-wing pilot for Christmas one year. It wasn't there.

I racked my brain to figure out something that would prove he existed and show he was missing. What else could I do? If Nick's own mother didn't know who he was, how could I convince anyone else?

I suddenly remembered what the Manager had said about debt. "He would have to work off his debt, and then he'd be able to reset his watch." *But what does it mean to be in debt?*

CHAPTER 15

FIND HIM

The last few weeks of school were miserable. We hadn't heard anything from Nick. Our parents still had no idea who we were talking about. Even our teachers didn't want to talk to us. We tried to ask Ms. James, but she refused to discuss it with us. However, we always felt unusually calm after we left her class.

Graduation was quickly approaching, and Cody was selected valedictorian. "I hate giving speeches," Cody exploded one day during PE. We had just finished running three miles. Mr. Deway gave both of us an extra-long distance to run since we were so fast. "What's the point anyway? Nick is gone. I'm worried about him. Why won't they tell us anything?"

"Calm down, man. I know it's frustrating," I agreed.

"I just don't understand. Why doesn't anyone know that Nick is missing?"

"I'm not sure." I gave my friend a comforting pat on the back.

The afternoon passed. As we were leaving school, Kelly approached us. "Hey guys," she shouted.

"Kelly! Do you know who Nick is?" Cody asked abruptly.

She sat down, a bit shocked. "Nick, I know several Nicks. Which one are you talking about?"

"Nick Carr. Our best friend. The one we are always with. He doesn't care about school, has five older brothers. Anything?" Cody questioned her.

"Hmm, doesn't ring a bell. Besides, you guys never hang out with anyone else. It's always been the three of us," she stated.

"Wait. Do you remember our English project when we reenacted *Lord of the Flies*? I played Ralph. You played Piggy. Cody played Simon, and Nick played Roger," I added.

"No. Cody played both Simon and Roger. That's why it was so funny!" She threw her head back, laughing.

"It's no use. It's almost like he's been erased." Cody slouched over with his head on the table.

"You guys are serious right now?" Kelly asked cautiously. "You really think there is someone else in your group?"

"Yes! Nick Carr. He's the one who first introduced you to us. You partnered up with him for the eighth-grade science fair. You kept complaining to us because he never did any work."

"No way. That was Brandon. Ugh, he's such a jerk. I can't believe he's the prom king." Kelly sighed.

"What else can we do? Can we try to talk to the Manager? He seemed scared of Mr. Malcolm. Maybe we can talk to him alone," Cody suggested.

"I agree. Let's go now. Kelly, you coming with us?" I asked.

"Oh, sure. It's not like we have much schoolwork left." Kelly stood up and followed us to the bus stop.

We rode in silence, wondering what our next step would be. When we got to the store, it was completely empty! All the posters were gone. Even the racks holding them had been removed.

The door to the Manager's office was closed. The decal that said "Power Store" was gone. We tried to peek in to see any evidence that it had been there.

"What are you doing here?" We heard a voice behind us.

We turned and saw a man wearing a SaveMart vest.

"What happened to the store that used to be here?" I asked him.

"What store? It's been vacant for the last ten years," the man answered. "Don't you think about vandalizing it. We're hoping to rent it out soon. Go on home, all of you." He shooed us off and walked away.

I quickly ducked around the back of the Power Store. My friends followed. We saw a door and tried to open it, but it was locked.

"Are we gonna break in?" Cody asked cautiously.

"Oh, brother." Kelly pushed me aside and grabbed a bobby pin out of her hair. A few seconds later, the door clicked open.

"Whoa! Where did you learn that?" Cody asked in awe.

Kelly smiled and walked in. Cody and I followed. Kelly reached into her backpack and pulled out a mini flashlight. The light showed the Manager's office completely empty. There was no trace he had ever been there.

"See if there's something that'll give us a clue." We spread out and searched. It was spooky how empty the room was.

"Guys, it's hollow under here." Cody stomped down where he was standing. Sure enough, it sounded like there was a cavern below. We searched for a crack in the floor. Feeling along the ground, I found a button and pressed it. The floor opened to reveal a staircase. I looked up at Cody and Kelly.

Kelly started walking down the stairs. Cody and I followed closely after. There was no light, except for Kelly's flashlight.

After a minute, we reached the bottom of the stairs. We found ourselves in a cubicle. There was a desk with a computer and one small light. A man was sitting at the computer, staring at the screen.

"Manager?" I asked, approaching him.

"Jay!" The Manager stood up and exclaimed, "My goodness, you can't be seen here. None of you should be here. Leave at once!"

"Not yet," I replied with equal force. "Where is our friend Nick?"

"Nick. I'm terribly sorry. I'm not, I don't know." The Manager stumbled over his words.

Kelly, Cody, and I kept slowly creeping toward him.

"All right, all right. I don't know much, but people have been disappearing. Some of our clients have just disappeared as if no one ever knew they existed!" He collapsed in his chair in defeat.

"But you can talk to the Owner, right?" Cody suggested.

"The Owner? Ha! I'm just the Manager. I don't even have a power, so I wouldn't be allowed in the training center. Now really, you cannot be caught in here. Take this. It may be able to help you." The Manager shoved a folded piece of paper into my hand. "Now go! Promise to never return. It's not safe. Please just go!" The Manager urgently pushed us toward the stairs.

Stunned and confused, Kelly, Cody, and I quickly ascended the staircase. We soon found ourselves again in the Manager's old office. As soon as Cody finished coming up the stairs, the opening in the floor closed. We all filed outside, squinting in the bright sun.

"What was *that* all about?" Kelly demanded.

"Do you believe him? Do you think he has no idea what's going on?" Cody asked me.

"I don't know." I reached into my pocket and unfolded the piece of paper.

All that was written on it was, "Find HIM."

"What does that mean?" Cody asked, reading over my shoulder.

I shook my head in confusion. The three of us trudged to the bus stop and waited for our bus. We got on and wondered what to do next.

CHAPTER 16

THE OWNER

The Owner reclined in his black leather chair, slowly petting his cat, which sat on the right armrest. In front of him was a wall full of screens, each displaying one person in a cell. Each cell contained a bot that was forcing the person to use his or her power. You could hear their groans and cries in the background. The Owner's eyes scanned each screen. Then he stood up and looked intently at one.

"Yes," he said ominously, "you will be a fine addition to my collection."

POWER DICTIONARY

Categories

Emotional:	affects emotions
Mental:	used for mental abilities
Natural:	affect the natural world
Physical:	affects the human body
Telecal:	used for distance
Animal:	ability to morph into any animal you've touched
Breathe:	ability to breathe under water
Care:	ability to cause others to care about something
Calm:	ability to calm down the people around you
Control:	ability to control anyone with your mind
Detox:	ability to remove any poison from yourself or anyone you touch
Disappear:	ability to make objects or people disappear or reappear
Dormeatas:	ability to eat while you sleep
Earth:	ability to move earth with your mind
Flight:	ability to fly any distance or altitude
Ghost:	ability to turn invisible and hover over the ground
Grow:	ability to cause anything you're holding to grow as big as you want

Halt:	ability to freeze anyone or anything by holding up your hand
Heal:	ability to heal the physical body. With one touch, you would be able to heal almost any injury
Hear:	ability to hear any conversation or anyone in the world
Influence:	ability to lead someone's decision making, can also act as a truth serum
Interesting:	ability to increase or decrease someone's interest in a subject
Light:	ability to increase or decrease amount of light in a room
Manipulate:	ability to mold plastic with your hands
Memory:	ability to accurately remember everything you've heard, seen or read
Negate:	ability to cancel any Power being used
Projection:	ability to make a projection of yourself anywhere
Strength:	ability to pick up more than the average human
Telecommunication:	ability to talk with people far away from you as if you were standing next to them
Telekinesis:	ability to move things with your mind without touching them
Teleport:	ability to travel by envisioning where you want to go, causes you to appear in the exact location by thinking or looking at a picture
Telepath:	ability to read other people's thoughts. With this ability, you would be able to read anyone's current thought.
Weather:	ability to control or recreate any kind of weather

Special Thanks to:

My husband for his never-ending support
My mom for patiently editing the story with me
Jesse, Ruby and Kate for being the first students to
read the story, give their ideas and suggestions
My friends, students and former teach-
ers who inspired many of the characters

ABOUT THE AUTHOR

Valerie Erickson loves reading, sewing, playing games and spending time with her husband and one-year old daughter. She gets her inspiration and motivation for her writing from her junior high students.